T0354872

The Chosen

Rohan Pavone

Order this book online at www.trafford.com
or email orders@trafford.com

Most Trafford titles are also available at major online book retailers.

Cover art by my multi-talented friend Gehrig Carlse

Note for Librarians: A cataloguing record for this book is available from Library
and Archives Canada at www.collectionscanada.ca/amicus/index-e.html

Printed in Victoria, BC, Canada.

ISBN: 978-1-4251-9046-0 (Soft)
ISBN: 978-1-4251-9047-7 (Dust)
ISBN: 978-1-4251-9048-4 (e-book)

*We at Trafford believe that it is the responsibility of us all, as both individuals
and corporations, to make choices that are environmentally and socially sound.
You, in turn, are supporting this responsible conduct each time you purchase a
Trafford book, or make use of our publishing services. To find out how you are
helping, please visit www.trafford.com/responsiblepublishing.html*

*Our mission is to efficiently provide the world's finest, most comprehensive
book publishing service, enabling every author to experience success.
To find out how to publish your book, your way, and have it available
worldwide, visit us online at www.trafford.com*

Trafford rev. 7/30/2009

 www.trafford.com

North America & international
toll-free: 1 888 232 4444 (USA & Canada)
phone: 250 383 6864 ♦ fax: 812 355 4082 ♦ email: info@trafford.com

Dedication

*This novel is dedicated to my parents
(and my sister Damiana, she insisted)*

Acknowledgements

Many people were very helpful while I was writing this novel and it is difficult to not acknowledge the people who provide the environment in which one is able to explore their desires to learn. I would like to thank my teachers Mlle. Jennifer Chan, Mrs. Sheila Stuart, Mr. Joseph Pelliccione, and Mrs. Anne Engelhardt, who have always encouraged challenges and more importantly, never discouraged them. To Mr. Gerard *Mac*Neil, my principal, who has to balance School Board requirements and individual student needs.

Special thanks to my siblings, Damiana, Sanjay, Michaela who had to put up with the many re-writes and endless conversations about "his book". But most of all I would like to thank my classmates Daniel, Gehrig, John, Joshua and Taylor who endured the torture of reading most of a first version of a first novel, yet had the class to comment positively; their encouragement gave me the needed strength to complete this novel.

Even with all of the help I received, all of the editing that did not catch the many errors in basic grammar, or plot and character development is mine alone.

Chapter 1

A radio was tuning into a station. You could hear the wiry scratches of the antique filling the room with feedback and static. It sounded like a high pitched rasping, like fingernails on a chalkboard. Finally, after some fine-tuning, voices could be distinguished through the speakers,

"Come in A2. Over,"

"A2 to HQ. Over," Between the pauses, an annoying buzzing could be heard.

"Did you get the plans? Over,"

"Yes sir, they've been sent to Mildus. Over,"

"Shh! Don't say the M word. It's HQ, you nitwit!"

"Sorry sir,"

"It's alright. I don't think anyone has tuned into our station yet. Over and out." The radio clicked off and the rasping noise ceased.

A tall figure stood up from the radio and simply said,

"Mildus, eh?" He clapped his hands in the darkness and beckoned his servant to come forward. The slave, however, shivered at the presence of his master. As the figures conversed, their breath condensed into water vapour, for the temperature had plunged in the past couple of hours.

"Squire, I need you to send a secret agent to Mildus. We need the Blavarians wiped out from the face of Xecwer before I initiate my

plan. Get the double agent to get in for some top secret information," the squire made a quick bow and rushed out of the room. The tall man walked to his throne and scratched his beard thoughtfully. He had been planning the destruction of this rebellion for several decades now. Nothing would be in between him and his path to victory. Soon, the whole universe would be under his command...*

"Whoa!" Ra'id sat up in his bed, beads of sweat running down his face. He soon realised he was back in his room, and was an ordinary boy from earth.

Oh, it was only another nightmare, he thought, I'd better get back to sleep. I wouldn't want to miss out on tomorrow.

He knew his nightmare would be very much at the top of his mind. This had been his fourth nightmare that month, usually being the same case; one man sitting on a throne questioning the other creature from the opposite side. He simply tried everything; self-hypnosis, meditation, but the thought kept seeping into his mind. The double-agent was a new twist to his recent nightmare. He could even see the sweat rolling off the inferior creatures head in fright. The nightmare had become detailed enough for Ra'id to see that these beings were not human. Could it be reality? Maybe it was a look into the future? Ra'id could not, however, seem to get over this recurring dream. After pondering his mind slowly and carefully, he slowly fell back asleep.

*   *   *   *

The next morning, Ra'id slumped out of his bed and got ready for the day. He was an eleven year-old boy with a husky body and a round olive toned face. He lived with his mother as an only child. Many books, knick-knacks, souvenirs and what-nots littered the hardwood floor. Most of the books that had been read the night before were set alongside his bed, but some items were odd artefacts he had collected. A few had been accumulated from a recent trip to the museum. One was a small fork-shaped twig tied to a silky string, making a talisman. It was made of rowan wood. Ra'id quickly recalled the memory of his trip:

Ra'id stood gazing at a marble tablet etched with the words:
'In medieval times, peasants often had the belief of the existence of witches. Some small towns had laws decreeing that if someone was caught boiling herbs or wildflowers, they would be arrested immediately. Typically, they would be burned after a quick trial.'
Ra'id looked up to see a wax figure with a pointed hat on her head and a crooked nose. She had her arms and legs tied to an upright wooden pole behind her back. Flames were lapping her feet from below. Even though the scene was made of plastic and wax, the pattern of the orange-red flickering lighting seemed to make the fire come alive. Ra'id looked up more attentively and looked into the eyes. He kept his stare as he walked up to his mom to move along. As he walked, her eyes seemed to follow him, as if she was looking into his being, his very essence. Fear struck Ra'id in the heart, knocking the wind out of him. He stopped in his tracks, grabbed a nearby railing to steady himself and took several deep breaths. His mother did not notice his change in complexion as she was engaged by the diorama of the medieval castle. He walked quickly to the panel talking of witches and read, *'They saw the witch was guilty if she floated when thrown into the water (arms and legs tied) but if she sinks, they'd concluded she was innocent. The ones who sank were never found again. The punishment of being a witch was burning. At the burning, the witch was tied to a long pole of rowan wood, a type of wood that supposedly caused searing pain when held against a witch. The sticks and logs used to make the fire would be of elder, a wood that attracts witches and which need to be burnt in order to be destroyed,'*

Later that day, Ra'id rushed into the gift shop and bought a thick twig of rowan wood strung into a talisman, and rushed back to find his mother...

Ra'id was very superstitious, even though he knew there was significant evidence disproving his beliefs. Even so, he couldn't help but keep the charm with him. For some unexplained reason, it gave him a sense of comfort,

"It's looks like I'm going to be busy this morning..." He observed the room in his pyjamas. Noticing the untidiness and shabbiness of his room, he quickly rounded up all of his lucky charms that warded off fictitious creatures and placed them in the drawer nearest to his bed. He then collected his school books and notes and hastily crammed them into his old schoolbag. Once the room was no longer scattered with objects, he noticed an inch of dust that lay on the floor. He grabbed a broom and gave his room a rough sweeping around the corners and under his bed. He assembled the dust into a dark grey pile piled several centimetres high. He shoved it into a corner and again glanced at the room. Some traces of the dust were still about; where you could see the hardwood showed him where the broom had treaded through the forest of mites, dust, and only heaven knows what else.

Ra'id noticed, near one bedpost, the remains of a melted, half-eaten, candy bar, possibly months old; even the various dust vermin had long lost interest in this succulence. Ra'id grabbed a pair of tweezers from his desk and prodded the decaying bar,

"This could be an interesting experiment," He snagged the wrapper and left in a plastic container on his desk. He dropped it beside similar containers that contained various bacterial environments.

The reason why he had bothered to give his room a clean up was because he was going to have two of his friends over for the whole day. And, on top of that, there was going to be a sleepover in his very unwelcoming room.

"Not bad, if I do say so myself," Ra'id said, satisfied. He rushed out of the bedroom, swung around the banister at the end of the hallway before ramming into a wall. He almost glided the flight of stairs. Ra'id very narrowly had caught his head on the low ceiling of the main floor, but ducked in time. The wall was fast approaching, but Ra'id couldn't stop himself. With a heavy thud, he smacked against the wall. Our reckless friend shook it off and, without learning anything the more recent experience, continued to run.

He couldn't wait for his friends to arrive.

However, that doesn't mean you can rush the preparation of a gourmet breakfast. Ra'id gathered the various things needed for it. A small breakfast of a corn cereal, chopped nuts, various berries, and a sliced banana was assembled with the expertise of a dorm matron, quickly wolfed down, and topped with a tall glass of freshly squeezed, homemade orange juice (squeezed by Ra'id the other night).

Ra'id's mother, obviously awake no thanks to Ra'id's not-so-lucky run-in with the wall, called from upstairs in her singsong voice,

"Up early, eh Ra'id?" He heard her shuffling to his room. She saw the rare neatness of it and, suddenly waking up, exclaimed, "You've cleaned your room! Finally! I thought the dust mites would have settled in along with cockroaches,"

I've got cockroaches too? Ra'id thought to himself.

Though excited about his day, Ra'id was quiet for the rest of the morning, because both of them knew that Sunday was a day of rest for the two of them. The doorbell released two tranquil notes. Ra'id turned off his Mp3 player. He rushed to the door and opened it.

They were his youngest friends, Yavin and Tala. Yavin was an athletic nine year-old boy, who was nearly as tall as Ra'id. He wore a yellow surfing shirt and green shorts, along with his favourite running shoes. His sister, Tala was eight years old, and she was one of the tiniest girls around, but she had a lot of fight in her,

"Hey, Yavin and Tala, are you guys ready for the sleepover?" Ra'id asked with enthusiasm.

"I was scared at first, but then I thought about all the fun I was going to miss. So I decided to come," little Tala squeaked, hiding behind Yavin's bright shirt. She was shy and timid, but if she needed to, she would've picked a fight with the biggest person on the block.

"I'm ready. This will be my second sleepover yet! I'm so glad to have one at your house, and ~" Ra'id shut him up, annoyed by his constant babbling, as usual. So they hurried in and started the party.

An hour or so later, their game of Monopoly had unfolded into a grand scheme. Ra'id had hotels on several properties, mainly the red and yellow properties. He had a monstrous pile of fake bills in front of his lap. Yavin had splurged all of his earnings on Boardwalk and Park Place, which left his in the slums. Tala played a bit too cautious and had barely moved financial positions since the beginning.

The game wasinterrupted by the ring of the doorbell. Ra'id rushed to the door, who could it be? No one comes on Sunday, and we haven't invited anyone else except for... He opened it, and to his surprise, his other friend, Sasha was there. She was thirteen years old, tall and flexible and had long brown hair. She wore a baseball cap and had a yellow Survivors t-shirt. Her denim shorts matched her bag. Compared to her other outfits, she was a 'mess'.

"How did you make it?" Ra'id asked.

"Well, you see," she replied, "the other party ended up being cancelled, so I decided to come here and sleepover. I had nothing better to do." She thought it was all right to barge in the middle of a party and join in. But since she was Ra'id's friend and he remembered what she had done for him quite a few years ago, he allowed her to join. She walked in arrogantly and put her bag away and she joined them in the middle of the game.

Though it might sound like an odd friendship, this group had met up in daycare. Ra'id had just arrived, this being his first time away from his parents. Sasha saw that he was lonely and worrisome. She never had any friends, so she asked if she could play with him. Before you knew it, Ra'id was happy, and so they played at the daycare everyday. Then one day, Yavin and Tala came in as toddlers, who could barely walk. Ra'id decided to befriend them just like Sasha did to him. Those four friends grew up together, going to the same school and almost living on the same block.

As the day progressed from board game to board game, the sun had set and evening had arrived,

"Now that we've played every board game mankind has ever invented," Ra'id said to his friends while he packed up the game of Clue,

"I'll make some popcorn, and then we'll get out our sleeping bags and enjoy the show!"

They got everything ready within several quick minutes. The microwave, however, had burnt several dozen kernels. Nonetheless, Ra'id carried the bowl of popcorn upstairs, while holding the video 'The Fantastic Four', an epic sci-fi classic based on the original Marvel comics. It involved people flying around, chaos and destruction; one of Ra'id's favourite films.

They watched the movie for about two hours. Once the credits started rolling, Tala piped up,

"You know what? If I got to choose a super power I could have, it would be the power to transform into any animal. That'd be sooooooo cool!"

"Just to tell you, Tala, that movie is soooooo fiction. That means superpowers and all that stuff aren't real," replied down-to-earth Yavin, annoyed and embarrassed by his sister's foolishness.

"Oh, don't crush her imagination. She was having fun," shot back Sasha, "I mean; it would really be kind of cool to have awesome super powers," Sasha and Yavin got into a spat, as usual. Ra'id didn't bother interfering. Instead, he turned off the lights and got into his sleeping bag.

No one could sleep; everyone was too excited. They talked and talked about all sorts of things, trying to keep awake.

"I've got an idea!" Suggested Ra'id, thinking of the movie, "Why don't we think of super powers we'd like to have,"

"What the heck, I'll go first," said Sasha, "If I had a super power, what would it be…" she murmured to herself. Ra'id could here her strumming her chin as she thought.

"Aha! I know! I would have the power to turn invisible and to be extremely flexible." Announced Sasha, oblivious to the fact she chose two powers. "Gymnastics are getting tough nowadays, so a little extra help might be good,"

Girls, Ra'id thought, just strange.

His thoughts were quickly interrupted by Tala's squeaky voice,

"My turn! I would have the power to turn into any animal of my choice. With that power, I'd be able to understand animals even better than now. I want to learn all about them,"

"I'll go next," said Yavin in a mischievous tone, "Hmmm... let me think. I'll have the power to move things with electricity, or better still, have the power to control electricity," he let out a crisp, evil laugh, and added,

"Wait until my opponents on the track see what I have up my sleeve..." Ra'id read him immediately,

"Hey, that's cheating! I thought powers were for the good and pure hearted, not the evil," he recited like he read it from a badly written script.

Ra'id thought for a minute. When he thought this much, he stroked his chin often. He reasoned with himself that he'd grow a goatee in his future years to make it look reasonable.

"I know a much better power. It's the power to control the elements - water, air, earth and fire. That would be an awesome power!"

Ra'id looked at the glowing hands on his watch, realizing it was nine o'clock. "We better get to sleep, or my mother won't be so glad when she finds us sleeping in tomorrow," The four companions closed their eyes and fell silent pretending to rest. But, instead, they continued to dream of a world full of super powers.

*   *   *   *

The next morning, the alarm clock sounded. Everyone slowly crawled out of their plush sleeping bags that had become uncomfortably dampened from their sweat,

"Wake up! You'll be late for school!" Reminded Ra'id's mother from downstairs.

Everything was quiet for the rest of the morning. They got dressed in about an hour (four children using the same bathroom one at a time could take a while), brushed their teeth and packed their bags.

They hurried down stairs and wolfed down their breakfast of pancakes and sausages smothered in creamy maple syrup, and headed out the door with Ra'id's mother. Ra'id looked up to the house and thought, *Until after school, good ol' house of mine...* He despised going to school on Monday, especially after a great sleepover.

They jammed themselves into the minivan, and got out of the driveway. Ra'id's stomach suddenly felt uneasy. He always knew whether or not something was missing. He checked his bag for everything.

Pencils... Notebook... Binder... Textbook... Homework?!

"Mom, stop the car! I need to get my homework!" Yelled Ra'id. The car immediately came to a screeching halt. Ra'id opened the car door and ran out to the house. He opened the door, charged upstairs and searched through the papers on his desk. Some loose sheets flew out from it, but he soon found the assignment with his name one it. He sprang out of his chair and headed to the door. But, a blue ball, suspended in the air by an imaginary string, came into his path.

"What the... What is that?" Asked Ra'id as he reached to touch it. It was something he didn't understand, yet his curiosity lured him towards it. When his finger was in contact with the sphere, his mind went blank and his conscience simmered away quietly...

"*With companions, tap into the orb's powers, and control the Legacy of Power. Destroy the evil that lurks about searching for you, and let the balance of power calm. Hurry, time's short,*" said a soft soothing voice. *The vision slowly faded away...*

"Ra'id, would you just hurry up!" his mother cried from outside, "You're going to be late!" She didn't appreciating him being late because it would've, indeed, made her late too.

"Right away, Mom." He replied half to his mother and half to himself, still groggy from the experience.

What a dream. I must be hallucinating, Ra'id thought.

He hurried outside into the car and they rushed to school. The traffic was close to nothing because they were indeed very late.

"Darn it. I hate it when I'm late; I'll miss out on something." Ra'id complained.

"Don't look at me; it wasn't me who forgot their homework!" Said Sasha, the four companions hurried into the school. But once they set foot in the door, they noticed that the lights were not on. Sasha went to switch on the light switch in the hall, but they wouldn't turn back on.

"Strange…" Remarked Yavin,

All of a sudden, screams of surprise and joy filled the halls. They were shouting because there was a blackout. The janitor had exited the basement of the school and explained to the principal,

"All of the power has disappeared. We can't even use the generator.

"I don't think there'll be a point to go to the office," Tala said. They each dispersed into different directions and hurried into their classrooms to begin whatever lesson that would be taught that day.

Ra'id hurried to the back of the classroom. Everyone greeted him on his way there. He lay down his bag, opened it, and was astonished to see the interior was glowing blue,

"Now what?!" Ra'id said as he faintly remembered the vision earlier that morning. The glowing blue ball had followed him to the class in his bag! He reached inside to get his homework. As he did, he felt a strong pulse thumping a rhythm to his arm. He peered inside even more and saw the ball. It was pulsating so slightly and perfectly, similar to a heart of some sort. It kept a constant and complicated beat.

Ra'id murmured curses to himself half obligingly, knowing he was dealing with something he did not understand. He reached for his homework again and handed it in. He walked back to his desk, took out a book and began to read under the dim lighting of some candles. The class had fallen down to a hushed tone that morning because nothing seemed to happen.

Ra'id couldn't focus on his book, however. The ball was stranger than anything he's ever seen or heard of. He decided to hide it in the case it might actually be something from out of this world. Scientists would want to test it. If they did, it could be chopped up and dissected. Ra'id shivered at the thought.

When the Vice Principal walked in and announced that it was recess (the bell didn't work because of the blackout), everyone dropped their books, and ran out the door and into the yard. Ra'id thought they could toss the ball around for the little while they had outside. However, he felt it pulsing in his palms, which reminded him that this was probably living. He decided to hide it under his shirt, but knew his friends had the right to know about it.

The yard was huge. It had a two hundred metre track, a soccer field, a playground and a cement playing area with basketball and hopscotch courts. Kids from ages six to fourteen ran, screamed and played in the field. The children had invented many assortments of games, usually involving a ball and a piece of cement.

Ra'id met up with his three companions. Nobody criticised him about having friends from different grades because he was a respected student in the class. Whatever he would do would be cool or Ok, never lame or immature. This wasn't because Ra'id necessarily cool, but his classmates were just mature kids. Anyway, his friends described what had happened that morning in their various classes. Tala's class didn't do anything because it was so dark. Yavin's class had gone out for a walk on the gloomy day.

Ra'id's class read under candle light. And Sasha's played board games. They hurried into the field of grass.

As Ra'id took out the ball to toss, Yavin noticed it was different,

"Where did you get that ball? I've never seen you with it before," He came a bit closer to see it, "Why is it glowing blue?" Ra'id explained what had occurred that morning when he had gone back into his house to get his homework.

"Are you sure you weren't just dreaming?" asked Sasha inquisitively.

"I'm ninety nine percent sure that the vision was because of this ball," Replied Ra'id, as though that extra one percent mattered. "The dream also said something about abilities – powers if this ball is properly used…"

A strange force pulled them towards it. They tried to feel if it was different, or if they could feel a force around the ball. Nothing was strange, however, about its texture; it was the same as any soft ball around. They all touched it and felt its texture, but, as all of their hands were in contact with it, it glowed even brighter, and, with one giant pulse, they were sent flying backwards, away from the ball, as if a giant shockwave had forced them back. They held their stomachs, winded from the shock.

"Get that cursed little ball away from me!" Shouted Sasha as she crawled away.

Yavin pointed out,

"We better line up, I heard the Vice Principal call us in." They hurried back to their lines and into the school.

Once they were in the school, they noticed the lights were flickering again. Soon they flickered into a bright light frenzy, and they shining brighter than ever before. The students filed through the hallways of the school back to their class. Back in Sasha's class, the students in eighth grade prepared for their French class.

"It's really strange… I mean, with all these lights going out, then all of sudden, they're shining better than when they were bought," remarked Vivian, one of Sasha's Grade eight friends, as she stared at the lights while talking to Sasha. She looked at Sasha to say something, but Sasha had already walked away.

How rude. She walked away from me while I was talking to her! Thought Vivian,

"Sasha, I wanted to say something, so could you come here?" Yelled out Vivian, thinking Sasha had stepped out of the classroom.

"I'm right here! I've been here for a while waiting for you to say something!" Sasha's voice yelled back to Vivian.

"What!? I can't see you! I can hear you but where are you?" Vivian asked.

"I'm right in front of you!" repeated Sasha, "You must have looked in the light for too long." Vivian blinked a couple of times and then she, after all, saw Sasha.

"There you are! First the lights start shining as bright as they can, and then you disappear! Talk about mysterious events," Sasha opened her mouth in astonishment,

"I was in front you the whole time. I think you need glasses. Stop looking into lights. That'll save your eyesight."

"Never mind," said Vivian, still confused.

"We should go back to our desks." The two girls headed towards their desks as the class began.

The school had ended earlier that day because several light bulbs had blown their fuses. Everyone gladly packed up their belongings before they exited the school. Ra'id's Mom was at an important conference, so he decided to take a ride home with Yavin and Tala. They took five minutes to get to Ra'id's house,

"Thanks for the ride!" He said as he waved back at them. Little did he know that he was in for a troubling week.

He turned the doorknob, and, to his disappointment, it was locked. He sighed heavily and sat down on the step, waiting for his Mom to return. Suddenly, he felt this strong jerk in his knapsack. He unzipped it to find the blue sphere glowing at an intense rate. His hands started to feel the heat radiating from it, and he released it,

"Augh! What the heck is wrong with this thing?" Before it could fall to the step, it caught itself, and hovered.

Energy flowed into it like a river pouring into the ocean. Various mosses and weeds wilted at its presence. The green chlorophyll of the leaves soon disappeared. Ra'id felt this sucking coming of him too. His vision shimmered occasionally, and knew his fate was set in concrete. He took cover behind the nearest tree, seeing if that would protect him.

The orb started to slow down now. Its glow resumed it usual blue hue, and the pulsing returned to normal. The ball stopped hovering and fell limp in Ra'id's hands.

Ra'id heard a 'click'. He went to the door slowly, very dizzy from the near death experience. He turned the doorknob carefully, hoping it was unlocked. To his amazement, it had swung open freely! He grabbed his bag and settled inside after locking the door again.

His mother had already made him some dinner. He popped it into the microwave and heated it up. It was a very delectable piece of food; a gourmet chicken salad. It had ground up leftover chicken, some raisins, and chopped walnuts. Ra'id tossed in two pieces of bread into the toaster and got to work. The microwave made a 'ding'. Ra'id opened its window and found the meal was steaming. He removed the toast from the toaster and took out a butter knife. He took a scoop of the chicken and spread on a piece of toast. On the other piece, he had put a bit of mayonnaise, and green piece of lettuce. In the end, he had a beautiful gourmet chicken salad sandwich. After devouring the meal, he chugged down a glass of homemade orange juice. Instead of being yellowish like the store bought kind, this orange juice was sweetly orange and full of pulp.

After clearing up his mess (every gourmet makes a mess after eating and cooking), Ra'id dragged his school bag up the stairs. He strung it across his chair and got to work. However, he had put the blue ball away in a shoebox, so no one would discover it, or, more importantly, so that it wouldn't discover anyone. He skimmed through the novel he was supposed to be reading, and then finished some homework assignments that were due in a week or so; it was just his nature. He quickly shoved his books back into the bag and went straight to the ball.

He removed it from its shoebox slowly, afraid that it might pounce at him, for some unknown reason. He took some droppers and put the ball on a sheet of paper on his desk. He began to test this thing. He put some drops of water on it. They quickly evaporated after several seconds of contact. Ra'id felt this sphere several times, and noticed nothing strange.

I guess it was my imagination. He thought in a small voice.

Suddenly, the ball noticed it was free from his grip. It sprang of the desk and into the air. Ra'id noticed its blue aura bouncing against the wall in front of him,

"What the ~" The ball came near Ra'id. He jumped for it, but it stayed suspended in midair. So it was something different. Ra'id tried to slow it down, but it was too fast. Ra'id was trying to outwit this living being.

What do I know about it? Oh, right; it can float, unlock doors, evaporate water, suck the energy out of anything it sees, and heaven only knows what else! It ricocheted off the walls, knocking things out of place. It was dark out, meaning the blue light would be flashing all over. Ra'id quickly closed the curtains when he heard a knock at the door downstairs. The ball stopped its chaos, and floated slowly to the shoebox. Ra'id, not knowing what was going on, simply covered it and went to answer the door.

"How was your day Ra'id?" His mom asked him as she walked in. Ra'id didn't bother answering. She settled her things in the kitchen and began to eat. Ra'id rushed to his room and tried to find the ball. He removed the shoebox and told it,

"You made this mess; so clean it up!" The ball floated in the air. It began spinning around like it had before. However, he didn't feel like the energy was being sucked out of him. It seemed like the ball didn't want to hurt Ra'id. Or maybe it was because the organisms that lived in his room had enough energy to clean it up.

Ra'id looked at the room. It was untouched. It had looked like the ball was never there. Ra'id let out a sigh of relief and settled the ball on the desk,

"Whatever you may be, you will not go crazy and create messes like that. You will, instead, follow me around for a while until we find something for you. Got it?" The sphere let out a greenish glow, as if meaning 'Yes'.

"Good. Now, into your shoebox. I'll have to find some way to contain you…" The sphere floated to its box and settled down quietly.

Ra'id had been right. Whatever it was, it was alive, and it could think. It breathed like a living being. However, it was unnaturally powerful, and could have destroyed Ra'id within a blink of an eye. Whatever it was, it needed Ra'id for some strange reason. Whatever it was, Ra'id knew that his future was going to be drastically changed because of it. Ra'id fell to sleep uneasily, knowing that he was harbouring something he didn't quite understand…

Chapter 2

"Well, slave, did you send out the double agent?" The tall figure's voice was excited now, for his reign over the universe would soon begin.

"Yes sir. We have sent 'em out to go and destroy the rebellion,"

"Very good. Now, where is the Power Orb? I must see it at once…" The being said. His eyes glinted in the moonlight like a dog's dark eyes. He waited quietly for the other to return. Within several minutes, the man came back in a slower-than-normal pace,

"Sire?"

"Yes…" He hissed. The tone the being used wasn't quite what you'd call 'joyful'. It was more like a 'we've hit an iceberg, captain' sort of tone.

"The Orb is… missing…" He said quietly.

"WHAT?!" The being's eyes lost its glow and rose from his throne.

After taking several moments to compose himself, he spoke in a calmer tone, trying to control himself,

"I didn't hear you properly… Could you repeat that?!" The room was filled with a light glow. It came from a staff the being was wielding. This was no friendly glow. The slave murmured quietly, choosing his words carefully,

"The… Orb is … missing…" He cringed in fear right after that. The being raised his staff from the ground, then smacked the bottom

of it against the floor. The slave scampered across the room, trying to find an escape. In a second, the staff filled the room with a blinding light. Energy spun in a wild vermillion bolt that danced around the room. The slave was, indeed, doomed.

When it had faded away, a pile of bones lay in a heap where the slave was. A janitor had arrived almost immediately and was ready for service,

"Clean up please… " The being had simply said, and then added, "Congratulations! You've been promoted…" The concierge let out a groan.

Ra'id was back in bed, five days after the discovery of the ball, having another restless night. His nightmare had been interrupted by some violent shaking from underneath his bed. Ra'id flipped to his side and removed the shoebox. The sphere came out and floated around quietly. Ra'id could hear it humming as it whizzed by,

"What's with you?" He asked softly so that his mother wouldn't hear him. Ever since Ra'id had had that nightmare, the ball would dance crazily around the room. Ra'id would wake up to the ball buzzing around his room. He would shut it up in his shoebox then clean up for breakfast. When he is about to leave, he would take it with his to school; it wasn't safe to leave it unsupervised, for some reason.

Strange things had happened the whole week. For instance, when Ra'id had left it alone on the day after its discovery, the room had been literally flipped upside-down. Once, he had to walk into his room that had become an anti-gravity chamber. So, he had decided it was safer to bring it along with him than leave it alone. Despite his antics, the sphere still got Ra'id into trouble. Once, during science class, Ra'id had to put his bag away in a locker. The orb must've acted up or something, because a nicely melted hole appeared on his locker door after class.

Ra'id had less and less ideas to keep this thing hidden. He knew that one day he had to reveal its secret to everyone. And when that day came, he would be ready for the worst, whether it was Ra'id protecting the sphere or it protecting him. Luckily, that day wasn't the day.

*   *   *   *

The week ended and the four friends were having a reunion over the long weekend. Ra'id hid the ball in his bag as he brought it to Sasha's house. They decided it was a nice day to go outside.

"Let's play hide and seek. There are so many places to hide. It will be a lot of fun," Tala suggested.

"Especially for the Seeker," Yavin replied sardonically. They quickly chose the seeker. It turned out to be Ra'id. He counted to one hundred by tens; who said you'd have to count all of that by ones! Sasha went to hide under some tall grasses growing in her yard, Yavin hid behind the house beside a drainage pipe, and Tala moved some mud into the shape of a burrow and hid inside. Once Ra'id finished counting he announced the standard phrase of hide-and-seek,

"Ready or not here I come." He turned around and opened his eyes. No sign of anyone.

This'll be fun, Ra'id thought as he walked around.

He softly patted the ground, wishing it could help him find someone. A sudden buzzing noise filled his ears. He clamped them shut with his hands, but it wouldn't disappear. He suddenly saw through the window of Sasha's house, and saw a soft blue light starting to shine ever so softly. Ra'id felt his energy being sapped out of him, like the other day, when he forgot his key. His senses began to blur, and time seemed to not matter now. Ra'id forced every ounce of strength in keeping himself together.

Ra'id was close to collapsing when the pain ceased. His whole body ached. On his knees in the mud, Ra'id held his head carefully.

That... hurt... too much... pain, were the only words he could force out of the messy state his mind was in. He eventually got up and looked ahead of him. His sight was returning, now.

The first thing that Ra'id noticed was that the ground had cracked up in front of him, revealing Tala. He jumped back, astonished by his discovery. The next thing Ra'id noticed was that everything looked different. The sky was bluer. The grass looked greener. But what scared Ra'id the most was that he could taste the air so well. He could taste the pollutants, morning dew, water vapour and various other things that seemed to hover in the air.

"B – b – but," Ra'id finally turned his attention to Tala, "How did you end up there?"

"I just had this sudden… urge, I guess," Tala replied. Ra'id, however, didn't buy it. Tala quickly changed subjects,

"Let's go find Yavin now! I think I saw him go around the side of the house." They both hurried and soon found Yavin, his back flat against the wall. Ra'id teased him,

"Nice hiding spot!" Yavin joined their small group.

They walked around, looking for Sasha, but she was nowhere in sight.

"Okay, we give up. You can come out now. You win," they all shouted out. She didn't come out. They repeated themselves. Sasha still didn't come out.

"Where are you? You already won! Come out, or we'll just leave you here," shouted Yavin.

"I've been here the whole time, right in front of you!" Sasha replied.

"Where? I can't see you…," Tala said. The grass was quiet and swaying with the wind, but it was very quite.

"I'm right here! Maybe if you squint, you might see me. I'm over here," said Sasha as she suddenly appeared.

"There you are!" exclaimed Ra'id.

"You guys definitely need your eyes checked," sighed Sasha as they walked down the street.

*   *   *   *

A few hours into their walk, after visiting a small burger joint to have lunch, not to mention a kiosk where Ra'id bought a piece of monkshood (to add to his charm collection), they reached a dark alley on their way home.

"I don't want to walk down this way," whimpered Tala. She clung on tighter to her older brother's shirt.

"No, I don't think want to either. We should turn back," added Yavin.

"You guys are such babies! There's nothing down here!" The others still didn't trust Ra'id. He turned his back to the alley and said,

"C'mon! I'm sure we went down this way on the way over. I bet you that the light is covered by the buildings from this angle,"

The others remained silent. They were looking over Ra'id's head and quickly stuttered,

"R - r - Ra'id? Behind y - you..."

"You actually think I'll believe that trick? That's the oldest one in the book~" He suddenly stopped ranting when an icy cold hand gripped his shoulder firmly. Its icy claws were slightly into his skin.

Ra'id drew all the courage he could to turn around.

A huge shadow blocked their path. The very tall figure that had slits for eyes stared down at them. His body features were all covered in shadow, which billowed slowly though to an imaginary wind,

"You're not leaving until you have helped me..." Ra'id turned around, wondering why his friends weren't helping him rip free of the man.

His companions were trying to keep themselves steady. The same pain that had overwhelmed Ra'id was overwhelming them. They lost their consciousness before Ra'id did.

Chapter 3

Ra'id woke up to a buzzing sound. And a headache. He struggled to get off the cold stone floor he was rested on. After steadying himself, he tried to focus. Once the room stopped spinning, he decided to walk. He looked around, and saw himself in a dank, dark room, with stone walls surrounding him. Abandoned cobwebs were each corner of the room. His friends were with him, but unconscious. He shook them awake, and, after several minutes of trying to steady themselves, looked for the source of the annoying buzzing sound. Besides his friends, nothing was familiar.

"My ears are hurting because of that... noise," complained Tala as they got up from the ground.

"Where are we? And how did we get here? It was kind of creepy when we turned around and saw that guy... the tall, shadowed one..." Ra'id could remember the vice grip of the claws gripping into his shoulder.

"I want to go home," said Tala, as she clung on to her older brother's shirt.

"So do I," responded Yavin, who was pretty scared too. They all huddled together in a corner. Shivers were crawling up and down their spines, but it had nothing to do with the temperature.

Along the opposite wall, from where the buzzing sound seemed to come from, the wall began opening slightly, revealing a dark hole. Inside, a black fluid substance could be seen, wavering to a non-existent wind. It sent chills down the children's spines to see such nothingness. A figure covered in a lightly billowing shadow emerged, gave a simple wave with his hand and the humming stopped. The children remained silent and immobile, trying to avoid the isolating gaze of the figure. Without paying any attention to them at all, the shadowy figure turned around, raised his hand up in the air and held his breath. Suddenly, the hole in the wall shrank, until it subsided.

He strutted through the room, and noticed the four of them huddled. As he turned to face them, Tala yelped,

"These are the beings the Power Orb was entrusted to? These despicable humans will be no match for what lies ahead." The being murmured to himself in a deep voice.

Only Ra'id dared to open his mouth, and none of his friends could believe he did it,

"Where are we? And what is a 'Power Orb'? Why have you brought us here? What was that buzzing sound? And – and take us home!" he stated matter-of-factly, as if rehearsing a foolish children's play.

The shadows around the being had hues of blue,

"You have courage; one of the many qualities to succeed at this perilous task. It isn't absolutely necessary, considering the fact you have other abilities, but your courage will lead you to victory. I can sense something great within you," the children had no idea what this useless gibberish was, but Ra'id sat down, not wanting to hear anymore.

"You are on the planet Xecwer," The being answered, "And a 'Power Orb', or should I say the 'Power Orb', is a source of miracles and greater power in this universe, including your powers. I brought you here, or should I say it brought you here to – to – to," The beings was trying to choose his words carefully, trying not to test the intelligence of the earthlings before him, "To

instruct complete controls of your powers and to master them."
He finished in an all-knowing tone.

Ra'id, completely astounded by what he had found out, spat
out questions off the top of his head,

"P – p – powers? It just doesn't make sense. I'm an ordinary
boy with ordinary friends. How could this have happened? Why
were we the ones to be chosen? Why did you choose me?"

"Now that you mention it, I ask myself that same question,"
Ra'id ignored the being and continued,

"Powers that can make unnatural phenomena happen is much
more than we can handle. It's just overwhelming. I can't believe
you," Ra'id said. As the last phrase escaped Ra'id's mouth, a
huge claw jumped from the shadows, grabbed Ra'id and lifted
him ten feet off from the ground. "Or maybe I can." He added
sheepishly. The claw dropped him onto the floor and retreated
into the shadows.

"As I was saying," the being cleared his throat, "You wished
upon powers, and they have been granted to you useless little
humans. You maggots have a great destiny, and you were chosen
by the Orb." Ra'id never getting the point, shouted,

"But we don't have an Orb!"

"It's the ball, you doofus! Get it through your thick skull!"
Ra'id remained quiet after this comment. His friends didn't crack
a grin, frozen by fear.

"It altered your atomic builds; now, your cells can alter pure
energy, also known as 'ether', and produce most types of natural
energy and more. You're now Catalysts." He took a deep breath,
allowing the children to take all of this in, and continued, "These
powers are activated when specific emotions are triggered. I am
one of those few beings who were entrusted with the power of
the Orb; I can control light. However, I alter light to create other
things, mainly shadow. I've never learned to control light itself,
so shadow is what I know best. When I am angry, the shadows
around everybody get hot, and I can create illusions of shadows

without a problem, such as the one I used to shut your trap," the being gave an austere glance to Ra'id, then continued talking,

"The people who do not control the power entrusted from the Orb can use its power, only if it's at hand. Enough of that. Now, on to finding your true power. Let's start with you," his shadowed finger pointed at Tala, who was cowering behind her older brother's shirt,

"Me?" She whimpered.

"Yes, you. Your power, or so I heard from your very lips, is to transform into any animal," his voice softened, "Now, can you think of the way a cat might feel," Tala thought hard for a moment, trying to hold back tears. She was under too much pressure to handle. But, she obeyed with a simple nod. The three friends were staring at her, waiting for something to happen.

Then something did happen.

Tala could feel her energy being sapped as she tapped into her power. A part of the brain that had not been used for thousands of years by humans was suddenly awakened. Like an old friend, calm thoughts from this part of the brain coaxed Tala on. She could feel that she could do it. With one final effort, Tala focused every brain cell she could on to the task at hand; think like a cat.

It happened within seconds. Tala began to crouch, suddenly shrank, and the process began. Where Tala used to be, a grey cat stood, mewing cautiously.

"S – s – she did it! How's this possible?" Ra'id was amazed at the proven evidence that what the being had said was not balderdash.

"Excellent. You also have the ability to read the minds of animals, and, if you touch them, you can absorb energy from it. Now, turn back to a human. Think the way humans think," Tala became her human form again within a blink of an eye. She slowly looked at herself to see if she was completely human and no longer a feline. Her hand fell upon her neck and she screamed,

"Ah! My neck!!! It's covered with fur!" The being in shadow simply shook his head,

"I was afraid this would happen,"

"Thanks for the warning!" Tala cried.

"Well?! What're you going to do about it?! My sister can't just waltz into her house looking like a leopard cub, with this tuft of fur and all!" Yavin yelled back at the being.

"I guess you'll have to live with it. There's no way to put it right. It'll stay there," Tala let out a deep sigh and subsided into the shadows, wanting to hide from her friends.

"Don't try that again because I forgot to tell you about restrictions. If you use your power too many times in sequence, you'll feel tired and limp. If you don't leave enough energy for your usual body functions you could," he hesitated,

"Die,"

Ra'id grabbed his throat protectively.

Yavin was the next victim,

"You're next. Your power, as I recall, is to control electricity. Now, try and feel the power within you. Think of being as energetic as electricity. Let it flow from you," Thinking Yavin had tapped into it, he continued, "Now, pull out your electricity and destroy this block," a block leaped from the shadows, with hues flickering like flames.

Yavin thought for a while, remembering his last science class. Blue electricity is the strongest and the hottest. He tried to get the energy to flow from inside him. Suddenly, his muscles began to tingle lightly. His brain suddenly began thinking faster, going faster than ever before. A certain part of it quickly forced the body to contain the power.

Energy coursed through his entire body, giving him new vigour. He took back his hands, and threw them forward. A beam of blue electricity shot out from his hands and destroyed the block of shadow.

"Ow! It's hot, and it's burning!" Yavin yelped. He was shaking his hands vigorously, trying to cool them down.

"When will they ever learn?" The figure murmured to an imaginary being above him in the ceiling, "You know you can control electricity,"

"Yeah, and?" asked Yavin, who had managed to cool his hands by slipping them in between some loose stones.

"It doesn't mean you're completely immune to it. If someone where to jam their finger in a battery, the electricity would burn them 'cause of the heat it gives off. You shot the electricity from your hand. Luckily, your power prevents any damage from what you control, or I'd be busy trying to scrape your melted hand off the floor." The being had finished and Yavin simply said,

"I'll keep that in mind," and he tapped his head with his finger.

He turned towards Sasha.

"Now, relax yourself. Your power is to become invisible and to be truly lithesome. Breath in and out slowly," Sasha took a deep breath as she was ordered and let it out, and the being continued, "Now, reach for this ball over here," a dark ball appeared from a thin shadow on the other side of the room. Sasha relaxed and waited. The ball floated ominously on the other side. She pulled her hand forward and reached, and stretched her arm as much as she could, while trying to relax.

Something started tearing at her triceps. They seemed to fall apart slowly, as if an organism of some sort beyond comprehension was at work, making them less stable. She ignored the pain and glanced at her hand. It had begun advancing slowly, which astonished her very much. She jumped back, thinking it was just a dream. Suddenly, her arm fell to the ground, still extending. It was stretching, but wasn't straight. It looked almost as if her hand was melting.

"Ahh! My arm! I – it's just stretching, like there's no bone in it!" Exclaimed Sasha, still freaked out by the fact that her hand was a melting mess in front of her.

"Yes. Some minor problems can occur while using your powers. You didn't believe your hand was stretching. It scared you a bit, which caused some adrenaline to flow within you. Adrenaline kills the enzymes that are containing the chemical reactions in your arm. It very complicated." Sasha was still panicking, regardless of the being's words. "Relax. You've got to trust me on this." Sasha slowly calmed herself and listened well, though no one could ever trust their abductor. Suddenly, her arm regained shape and retracted back to normal size. Once again, Sasha attempted to reach the ball. Her hand reached for it, but simply passed through. The ball had already disappeared.

"Nice work," said the being, clapping his shadowed hands, "Now, relax even more, without flexing. See what you can do, or should I say don't see." Sasha didn't understand what he meant. However, she relaxed even more and waited. The same felling tore at her body, taking it apart even more. A minute into this, she saw her friends gaping at her. She ignored them and waited. Her muscles felt cramped for an instant. After this, she felt like she was floating. She looked at her arm… and saw nothing at all.

"Wh, wh… Where is my hand," she looked around her whole body, "Where is my body?" The being started to explain,

"You've become invisible. The protons of your atoms have stretched further apart from each other, though still orbit around each other, therefore making you almost disappear. Nothing can see you. This can be stopped once adrenaline starts running through the blood, or the air, I could say. So don't be afraid if you want to hide, but, instead, relax." The being finally turned to Ra'id and said, "You're my next target."

"Your power is to control all of the~" Ra'id interrupted,

"Elements. I know." The being continued, trying to contain his anger,

"As I was saying, before this rude human interrupted, he can control elements. To control the elements, it seems as though you need to control your emotions. Different emotions trigger certain elements," The being stopped when he saw a light illuminate from the corner of his eye. He turned to see Ra'id snapping his fingers. He snapped it once and a single flame danced from his finger. It flickered back and forth. The being cleared his throat. Ra'id forced himself from his fiery snapping and looked at up at the being. His flame flickered out and he said,

"Sorry, just a bad habit of mine..." The being ignored this fib, and continued,

"As I was saying, earth, wind, water and fire are the most basic of the elements," Ra'id threw a droplet of water into the air, which collided with a ball of concentrated air. They connected and made a mist.

The being cleared his throat once again. Startled, a thick stream of hot mist shot of Ra'id's hand, headed straight for the being. He waved his hand ever so slightly, causing something to leap from the shadows and take the hit. The mist sizzled against the shadow, which retreated quietly into a dark corner.

"However, unknown abilities have yet to be discovered. Combinations of emotions will trigger your abilities. Courage, of course, is one of the most complicated emotions, along with depression, and love," Ra'id pointed his finger to his open throat and imitated a vomiting motion.

Suddenly, the being disappeared and reappeared at the top of the room, "Now, come and reach me up here."

How about using a bit of earth get him. Ra'id felt the pain he felt at Sasha's. Energy flowed from within him, trying to organize itself. His mind took control. Suddenly, the earth began to stir from beneath him. He raised his hands, and brought them down quickly, clamped them together and pulled down on to thin air. At his command, fists of earth reached down and grabbed the being. He struggled slightly, causing Ra'id to strain his grasp. Then he slipped out. Though Ra'id was not successful, the four companions were amazed at how he had tamed his abilities so quickly.

"Nice try, but it'll be harder than that."

How about a hovercraft... of sorts... Ra'id began to draw intricate, imaginary circles around him. The air around him tightened beneath him, forcing him upwards. He reached for the being and touched him, who said,

"Well done, but you may not have had that much time to think about what you're going to do. I suggest you know your opponent's weaknesses before using any power at random. However, it is best to let your emotions take control of your powers. With it, you can do things you never imagined." They both descended to the ground.

He looked at each of the children, then said,

"Now to test whether you understand your cataclysms, I shall plan an encounter, a challenge, for each of you. The goal is to reach the void on the other side of this room," a black hole appeared on the other side of the room. It seemed to contain nothing but a silky, black fluid, stirring around quietly.

"Tala will start," Tala sheepishly walked to the wall opposite of the hole.

"Begin," implied the being. Tala walked cautiously across the room, keeping a stern stare at the fluid filled hole. She stopped in her tracks, her heightened senses acting before any of the others. Out from the wall jumped an animal covered in shadow the size of a wolf. Tala prepared to transform, but thought back,

He told me transformations take up the most energy of all the powers, so I should use it wisely.

Instead, she got down on four legs, trying to keep her ground. She was a shrew compared to the wolf. It was a meter tall when standing on fours. She kept sidestepping, and every once in a while, striking with her hand. The wolf tried to circle her, but she followed it around. It came closer, and wound its back legs, preparing to pounce.

Now! Thought Tala.

She extended her hand and struck the wolf. The instant her hand hit the wolf, claws extracted through her finger nails, which gave the wolf a large cut. The moment her claw touched the wolf, images flashed through her mind,

I'm a friend, not a foe. I'm only being territorial, thought the wolf as Tala read through its mind.

"I've got it!" Exclaimed Tala, as she ran on four legs towards the opposite side of the hole. She slowly inched across the wall, until she reached the hole, and jumped through it, almost to easy.

The wolf immersed itself into the shadows at the command of the being. He signalled to Yavin,

"Now, your turn Yavin." Yavin backed up against the opposite wall, ready to run to the other side. The being quietly said, "Begin," Yavin jumped off the wall and sprinted at full speed to the other side. Half way there, his vision suddenly grew dimmer. However, he continued, and collided into an object that felt like an iron wall. He fell back a couple of meters, airborne,

"Ow," he cried in agony as he rubbed his forehead. He ran forward once again and ran into the wall.

When he backed away, and a giant with square body parts covered in a billowing shadow appeared. Its fist was held up, ready to drop.

"Oh, man," Yavin said, as he waited for the giant to make a move. Its fist plunged down, catching fire while dropping at such a velocity. Yavin dove to his right, narrowly evading the fist. The impact from that punch shook the whole room, sending Yavin flying back,

"I'll show you how to push!" Yavin shot a luminous ball of white electricity from thin air at the giant, illuminating the room with a brilliant light. While the room stayed lit, the giants shadow dissolved away, revealing a metal ogre with square body parts stacked on top of each other. A dark blue shined against the wall, cast by the ogre's metal.

Yipe. In one false move and I'll be clobbered. I'd better think quickly, thought Yavin as he dodged another attack from the ogre.

The steel fist made a loud hollow sound as it struck the floor.

I know! I'll just need to bring it to the center... Yavin let his ideas flow as the ogre prepared another attack. Yavin ran towards the center of the room, and sprinted quickly in circles.

I need to be really energetic for a shock like this one, he thought as he kept running.

A small charge began building within him, and he had the sudden urge to release it while he was running,

"Not yet," he kept on saying over and over. He tingled all over, which disrupted his thoughts and actions. The ogre threw his hand down at Yavin. Once it was only centimetres away, he raised his hands like lightning and focused the energy into the ogre's hand. Extremely hot blue electricity escaped the inside of the fist and had caught a current on the metal. The electricity ran up the ogre's arm, too quick for the beast react. It left a trail of fiery sparks, causing the metal to melt away. The metal made a grinding sound as the hollow body of the ogre was split. The two pieces of metal lay still on the ground, white hot. Yavin felt a wave of exhaustion go over him, as he trudged towards the black hole and jumped through it.

The pieces of metal vaporised as the being said,

"Now you, Sasha," She edged herself against the opposite wall to the hole as calm as ever.

She thought very audaciously: This will be a piece of cake.

"Begin," said the being as the room suddenly became darker. The shadows in the room crawled along the stone walls. A shadow appeared out of nowhere in the center of the room, but it belonged to nothing. Sasha eased herself and she became invisible. The tearing feeling weakened her steadily. She walked across the room, waiting for the shadow to attack. It didn't. She headed towards the hole, tasting sweet victory in her mouth. As she drew nearer, the hole disappeared then reappeared to her right. She followed it more, and it kept on disappearing, frustrating Sasha,

"Darn this is so frustrating!" Said Sasha and she appeared. The shadow turned at the sight of Sasha and ran towards her. It raised its fist. Sasha dodged the fist, and ran back to the other wall. The shadow left her alone.

Let me try that again, but this time with an extra stop, Sasha thought.

She turned invisible once more and inched towards the shadow. It didn't notice her, so she extended her invisible hand to touch it. She grabbed its shoulder and focused. She relaxed as she thought of being relieved of all burdens. Sasha tapped into the being's energy supply, and quickly began taking its energy away.

The shadow suddenly became wearier, and it fell down on its knees and started shaking. After another minute, the shadow fell on to the ground, dead. Sasha felt re-energized. She headed towards the hole. It still moved out of the way. She, once again, got too frustrated, and became visible. That instant, the hole moved towards her, allowing her to walk through it.

"Wow. How come she gets the easy task? Nothing happened!" Complained Ra'id. The being said,

"If you became invisible, the whole world will change. Everything would look different. You could talk to spirits of animals and trees. Anyway, it's now your turn to try your luck at the task."

Ra'id walked up to the opposite wall, and waited. The being sternly stared at him and added, "Don't be so foolish this time. Begin."

An eight legged animal appeared in front of Ra'id. Its legs were spread out against the floor with a balloon shaped head.

Octopus. Tsk, easy, imagined Ra'id as he walked to the other side, without even noticing the invertebrate. It elongated its tentacles out towards Ra'id, though he didn't notice. Then, the octopus surrounded Ra'id with the tentacles, and started squeezing him.

"Ahh! The octopus is going to kill me!" Whimpered Ra'id and he struggled feebly to get out.

Can't... move... a muscle, thought Ra'id.

He could feel the same pain starting to act up again. Energy tingled in his finger tips. Suddenly, out of shear anger, Ra'id body erupted with fire. The inferno did harm Ra'id, though the eruption lasted a split second. He extinguished the fire that caught his clothes. The octopus had recoiled, its tentacles devastated from the attack. It seemed unharmed, because of the oozing liquid it was continuously shedding. Nevertheless, the creature took a more cautious approach.

"Ha! That hurt it. Now, if a little fire would help – wait! That liquid is protecting it from any damage. So let's see if the inside is as well protected," said Ra'id, as he built up even more anger inside of him. Then, he focused on the inside of the octopus. Instantly, flames roasted the octopus' heart, killing it within the minute. It rolled over, and green puss spewed from its blowhole.

Ra'id's legs felt like lead. In all the excitement, he trudged to the void and beyond.

*   *   *   *

Chapter 4

Ra'id felt his body being pulled apart. The tearing ripped his protons apart as they flew through the oblivion of nothing. His thoughts seemed to be the only things that hadn't been disorganized. Ra'id knew the end was coming near, for his atoms started being pulled together again. His body emerged in one piece.

The hole enlarged to the beings entrance. He closed it with his hand. Tala turned towards them.

"It's about time you came here. This world is beautiful," said Tala as she called over the squirrel.

"So, Ra'id. Do you want to go back to Earth now that you've seen part of our beautiful planet? That musty old manor is probably the most disgusting thing in the whole planet," questioned the being as he started gliding across the field. His tone of voice suddenly became a down-to-business kind of tone,

"Quick. Everyone follow me as I'll take you all to your home planet. With that training, I hoped you learned how to better defend yourselves," ordered the being as he beckoned them to follow. Ra'id stopped in his tracks,

"Defend ourselves from what?"

The being, too, stopped. He turned around to face Ra'id, and answered in a tone that probably wasn't supposed to be frightening but sent shivers down his spine,

"Things that seek you day and night that aren't from your planet…" and he left it at that.

The group remained silent for the rest of the walk. They came to a stop in front of a huge station, or at least what resembled one. It was quite odd to see so many animals following them on their route. The station was balanced on a thick pole at a 45° angle, with a huge platform placed on top of it. A large disc, shining in the sunlight, was tilted to its side, propped by three spindly legs. The whole structure was made of a fairly strong, yet light metal.

"This is where we part," spoke the being sorely.

"What? Where are we going?" asked Ra'id, puzzled.

"Well, don't you all want to go back to your home planet?" Replied the being as he started pointing to a dark blue spec in the clear sky,

"That is planet Earth. We had better hurry up before the ship leaves." He indicated lights running along the side of the dome, creating an incandescent pattern.

The whole group hurried up, mounted the long pole (Which turn out to be a type of stairs), and prepared to board the ship. As they drew nearer, a rectangle descended from the bottom of the dome. Hisses escaped the high velocity, aerodynamic apparatus, causing a cool breeze to fall upon our companions. Stairs come into view after the mist had dissolved. The being's thin purple eyes widened as he observed Earth,

"Mighty fine planet, you got there. But, this one is a lot more elegant,"

"What do you mean by… elegant?" Asked Sasha.

"Oh, yes. I forgot. You've never seen the beings that live here. They are more elegant than you lesser beings. They are more… evolved, you could say. Too bad you can't see them now that were leaving," continued the being. He gazed at the planet deeply, as if in a trance.

Suddenly, a black dot enveloped the planet, engulfing the blue spec. His cheery tones vanished with the spec,

"No, it can't be. Not now…" Rasped the being in a tone of desperation. The black dot moved away, and nothing remained any longer of the planet.

"What's wrong? We're leaving you! Why are you so sad?!" asked Yavin as he turned to the being.

"Y – Your planet – Is destroyed. Nothing remains of it in the sky," finished the being, as he turned sadly to the humans, where his shadows were a purplish tint,

"I am sorry…"

"You… You mean the planet is…" at this point, Tala started crying, "Destroyed?"

Ra'id felt emotionally cold inside.

My mom… Dad… everyone… all just… gone… Even though Ra'id hardly ever expressed his emotions, a tear splashed against his cheek. He felt alone, solitary and cold. His next tear rolled down his face, only to freeze into a droplet of water.

These powers… they'll force me to be emotionally controlled… I have to be a cold, heartless rock… The frozen tear quickly heated up and evaporated, then condensed into a tear again. His powers were freaking out with his emotions. He set his thoughts aside and contained himself.

"Yes, it is. It is grave indeed. This – This is the work of… King Crenar!" The being said as he held up his fist. He spat on the ground as he said Crenar's name.

"Who?" Asked Ra'id after wiping his tears away.

"The only being powerful enough to wipe a planet out is King Crenar. He must have heard that the Power Orb was on that Planet, so he decided to destroy it, so he could destroy whoever the powers were bestowed upon. Good thing you're already here, but now… You cannot return…" answered the being.

The children also had sorrowful looks on their faces, and they thought of what might happen if they were obliged to live there,

"We'll need to find a place to be hidden away from this King, before he finds you and eliminates us from the planet," Sasha said to break the morbid silence.

"Excellent idea, you all can follow me to the Blavarians," said the being, sounding cheery.

"The Bananerians?" Asked Yavin, completely perplexed, not to mention deaf.

"The Blavarians is a secret resistance against the Crenar. I," and the being said this proudly as he put his hands against his chest, "am the leader of the Blavarians. There are only six of which have such powers, besides me. I am the only one with powers from the Power Orb." The children did not understand this, but had no authority (or at least they thought) to ask questions.

"Well, we better hurry up before the King finds out that we weren't on the planet," suggested Tala, as they hurried down the station's port. Yavin took a leap of faith off from the platform. He magnetized himself to the station with the electricity. His body suddenly clung to the wall. He rubbed his head for a bit, and then shook his hands vigorously, for the heat had burned them.

"C'mon, guys! Try it!" Yelled Yavin from below, "Use your powers!" Ra'id understood at once. He ran around at break-neck speed, and leaped of the platform. Then, by controlling the wind, his energy controlled the air around him, focusing them into cushions of air. He used the cushions to make an invisible staircase as he descended to the ground.

Sasha was next. She tried to relax,

Ok, relax. I'm only going to jump off a platform a hundred feet from the ground. Nothing much, she thought sarcastically as she prepared to jump.

She preformed a cart-wheel and jumped the platform. As she got closer, her legs stretched out, and landed on the ground. Her legs dropped back to normal size, causing her to slowly descend.

Tala had it all planned out. She folded her arms against her back, and spread them over and over again. She crouched on her knees, and sprinted for the ledge. Once she was in the air, she spread her arms and legs, and looked straight ahead. Then, feathers began to grow on her body and arms. However, the tuft of fur remained. Her feet became scaly as they shrunk. A large beak protruded from her mouth, completing the transformation. She had become a bald eagle. She screeched and glided long ovals, using the heat columns rising from the ground.

The being slowly descended, for he could float, and glided across the plains. Ra'id glided in the air with Tala flying by his side. Yavin used his energetic power to sprint quickly, and he sometimes went too far ahead. Sasha took long strides with her elongated feet.

Suddenly, Tala stopped flapping her wings and glided on the spot. She let out a sharp shriek to warn her friends. The being also stopped and he held his arm over his ear,

"Quick! Everyone, you must go and hide! The gu ~" A sharp screech filled Ra'id's ears. His slightly heightened senses noticed the disturbance in the air.

A large sucking sound was heard, and a hole opened up out of thin air. Everybody stopped, and waited. Suddenly, a purple substance was shot at the being, paralyzing him instantly. Two figures with orange armour emerged from the void. They didn't seem to notice the children.

"Remember the orders, Snar'lig, to only take Raghouik and leave the humans for their fate," reminded one of the guards to Snar'lig. The soldiers, or brutes (not much difference here), grabbed the substance and dragged the being away. The children in the sky descended, as they prepared their powers. They heard the being say,

"Don't worry about me; take care of yourselves and inform the resistance," and he went through the hole of nothingness.

The children didn't know what to do.

"Let's start heading that way," suggested Ra'id, pointing to the direction they were initially heading to.

"There seems to be a strong current here of something unnatural... " Mumbled Yavin, as he reached towards the concentrated area. Ra'id, noticed a funny taste in the air. It was... metallic. Something that wasn't organic, he was sure. Yavin was drawn to where the energy was flowing from it. Suddenly, he felt the cool surface of a metal dome; however, nothing was in front of him,

"Strange," wondered Yavin, as he started sapping energy. The dome counter acted and sent a strong jolt of electricity through Yavin's body. He jumped back, "Ay! What the ~" A big hole opened in the middle of the sky.

"Not another one!" Cried Yavin and he ran to warn his companions.

"Guys, look over there. There's a floating hole in the sky..." whispered Yavin in awe. Without provocation, a loud voice boomed across the field, shaking leaves off the trees. However, the squirrels and chipmunks continued to watch and had not retreated.

"You shall never escape this planet, for you shall not even survive your first encounter of one of my minions! Actually, you might escape...however, probably not in one piece! MUHAHAHAHAHAHA!" Boomed the voice very maniacally. The hyper-active electrons on the outside of the ship calmed down. A large disk similar to a flying saucer appeared, as if it was hidden from view.

A rather pungent smell filled the air as Ra'id drew another breath. His friends didn't seem to notice the change in the air's smell. A gigantic shadow descended from the hole. It was about fifteen meters long, five meters wide, and two meters high. The traits of it became clearer as it approached. Two equally sized pincers exited the shadows, followed by several different round sections forming a mahogany shell. The sections were connected to a long body with thick legs like tree trunks. These, too, were divided into many sections. The children suddenly became aware when a sword-like stinger hung above the monstrous body that came out of the shadows, followed by a thick extension divided into many sections. The children saw it attached to the body. The image suddenly struck their minds.

It was a giant scorpion! But in reality, it was a breed of an invertebrate and vertebrate, causing it to develop an internal skeleton along with an exoskeleton. Over the thousands of years that species existed, the skeleton allowed it to grow to monstrous sizes, resulting with a monster that could seal the children's fate.

"Perfect. The one time the Raghouik, or what's his face isn't here, we have to fight for real," exclaimed Ra'id in disgust,

"Well, here's the plan…" They discussed for a while then,

"And if that doesn't work…" and they made a back-up plan, though they doubted it was needed. The scorpion had reached them within minutes, despite its slow pace.

"Now!" Ra'id burnt the grass beneath it, which angered it. Then, Yavin began speeding around it. The fire picked up and caused a towering cyclone to encircle the insect (of sorts). The scorpion lay trapped. Fire clashed against the scorpion as it began to feel uncomfortable with the extra heat. However, the hard shell surrounding it kept it protected from the heat.

As the fire cleared, the scorpion threw its stinger forward. Fortunately, it struck the soft ground in front of it. Yavin picked up the dirt with his speed, and a cloud of dust engulfed the scorpion. It flailed its claws all over as the stinging earth wormed its way past the armour and stung its soft interior.

The confused scorpion thrashed its dagger into space, seeking a target. The stinger itself missed, thought the clubbed tail hit someone. Yavin to be exact. He flew backwards from his speeding frenzy and landed with a hard thud. He skidded along the ground and remained still.

The scorpion's task was to kill the Catalysts. However, that's like asking a bull to do an assassin's job; the scorpion was all muscle and no brain. So, in the end, the most the scorpion could do was knock them unconscious, which could do a bit of damage. Yavin will be safe, for now.

That rampant scorpion will no doubt stomp on him, Concluded Ra'id.

His thoughts were interrupted by a cry. More like a squeak, but, nonetheless, a cry.

"Ra'id! You've got to protect Yav~" Tala was quickly swept aside by the monster's claw, like a human does to an annoying gnat, and fell limp. A few bones would've been, without a doubt, broken.

Two kids – Catalysts – versus a giant scorpion that had hardly enough brainpower to light a filament. This is going to be close Ra'id thought sarcastically as he sidestepped a lunge. He noticed the vulnerability of his friends,

"I've got to protect them…" He forced their bodies underground and buried them with lightly packed soil.

Sasha was annoying the scorpion most effectively, if slapping the beast counts. And, when something is annoyed, this annoyance fuels it with the want for bloodlust; the need of seeing blood. Therefore, the scorpion began to a stabbing frenzy. Sasha stretched her invisible body away from the stinger.

It was when Ra'id noticed that the scorpion was attacking a certain empty space in the air that their luck changed from bad to worse. Of course, having your particles stringed away from each to appear invisible has its advantages; not being seen is one of them. The disadvantage is that your volume decrease, which means you become lighter than usual. A single gust of wind could send you spiralling out in the world. Or even a stinger the size of a sword attached to a club-like end could. Sasha noticed she was drifting off in the field. The scorpion didn't notice it was doing so.

Sasha rematerialized from thin air. The scorpion lunged in her direction,

Prey. Kill. Eat, were most likely the things that it was thinking, though it may have been slightly more primitive. Whatever the scorpion was thinking when it saw Sasha didn't affect the outcome whatsoever, Sasha dove to the left, and the stinger, laced with anaesthetic, grazed her calf. It acted immediately and threw her unconscious.

Ra'id stared in awe and in fear as the scorpion delivered the blow that left him alone. He felt fear crawling up his spine, causing him to send a chilly mist of ice crystals. His emotions would do basically everything. But maybe not everything he needed to decimate the scorpion. Or so I thought.

I re-examined the facts that came from the interviews, and it seemed quite impossible. It was when cogs in Ra'id's started to turn that the scorpion lost its advantage of size.

The ice crystals were slowly melting in the humid air, fuelling Ra'id's mind with ideas,

I could try freezing it… Nope, too much risk; I'm hardly able to contain my basic powers, let alone the complicated ones. And besides, arthropods can resist lower temperatures because they have anti-freeze in their blood… alcohol is the exact term, Ra'id noticed that he started to sound a lot like his science teacher, who droned on and on about a single subject for hours on end.

Ra'id's thoughts slowly drifted back to the scorpion, who lunged at him. Ra'id dove to the side. He quickly rose several stone pillars, about his height, around the scorpion, who couldn't tell which was Ra'id. It started walking towards each one, bashing them down one at a time, giving Ra'id time to think.

Anti-freeze… alcohol… Wait! I can probably fry the scorpion! Since the alcohol's mixed in the blood, the boiling temperature would be… He ran a few vague calculations. The chances of him succeeding before he fried up were slim. Nope. The temperature for that would be difficult to reach with such a shell, unless I got closer… Another idea came, but it, too, was shot down. The scorpion would overheat at a much later temperature than me… I guess. His own heat would eventually fry him, even if they were at such a low temperature (relative to fire, that is).

The first step of his audacious plan was the most dangerous part; he needed to cling onto the scorpion's underside to transfer such a small amount of excess heat. The scorpion had bashed the effigies of Ra'id onto the ground and noticed the last one standing in the field. Ra'id had tossed a fireball between the strong plates of the scorpion to draw the scorpion's attention from the prey it was about to feast on; Sasha. However, an annoyance stood between it and its meal, and it needed to remove it.

Usually, anything in their right mind would back away from a two tonne scorpion roaring them down. Then again, Ra'id wasn't anything at all. He was a loyal friend, not to mention a Catalyst. The scorpion was confused and saw that its victim was not losing his ground, so it had to take several moments to think. Ra'id continued to fire different thing in his arsenal until he regained the scorpion's attention. In a fury of rage, it struck with vermillion speed with its stinger. Ra'id carefully sidestepped and didn't hesitate to execute his plan.

He dashed around the scorpion's chewing parts and ducked under it. He quickly clung himself onto the loose plates of the scorpion. He dug his nails deep into the flesh to keep its attention. The scorpion screeched in pain and searched the ground for the pain. Of course, it was difficult to crane your neck underneath your chest, especially if it consisted of three strong plates. The idiotic scorpion spun itself in circles with unknown dexterity, searching for his next meal.

Ra'id hadn't anticipated this at all. Then again, Ra'id hardly anticipated anything. He held onto the scorpion, and most importantly, his stomach. It was time to initiate the second step in his plan.

Ra'id used his powers to his advantage. He gripped the bottom plate of the scorpion tightly. He pried his arms as deep as he could under the plate, trying to reach the center. When he could not reach any more, he let his emotions take over;

I will succeed... this thing will die... He felt his muscles tighten. They grew rigid within seconds. In their place were stone arms that had attracted the earth towards them for cover. With the added weight, he crushed the plate in a bear-hug squeeze. The bare skin of the scorpion was revealed. The shards of the exoskeleton lay to his side. He shook his hands clean of the clumps of dirt that stuck to him.

Using his arms as best as he could, he clung to the plates on the outside of the bare space. Ra'id wedged his shoes beside the plate and scorpion to get a good spot to heat up.

Ra'id began to raise his body temperature. It was difficult for someone with very little control with his powers, so maintaining a constant temperature was vital. He focused with all his might to lift his body temperature. All he needed was to raise his body temperature to a decent forty degrees Celsius. Of course, he would feel a bit more than feverish, but the scorpion will feel it worse.

Then again, the chances of that were very low indeed. Ra'id didn't know what the adverse affects of heating of the scorpion was. He needed to start heating up slowly, allowing his heat to trail into the scorpion. Energy ran down his fingers as the ether transformed into heat energy. It surged down his arm and into the scorpion's body. These spontaneous bursts of heat would eventually heat the whole body. That was if he survived that long.

He felt woozy within five minutes. It was either the spinning or the heat that kept him nauseous, but, either way, he wouldn't last any longer. The scorpion was, in fact heating up. Ra'id could feel its body temperature rise. Being cold-blooded, as the scorpion was, allowed it to resist build ups of temperatures by adapting too it. Ra'id was hoping that the increase was at a steep enough pace to remove the scorpion.

A sudden surge of uncontrolled energy scurried down his arms and into the scorpion's body. It was automatically transferred into heat. Ra'id's fingers couldn't stand the scorching, and lost his grip. The scorpion, however, felt the heat blast through its body, which was unaware for an incline of heat such as that. The recent heat wave surprised the scorpion's body.

Ra'id quickly noticed that the scorpion was loosing its balance. He rolled to the side and ducked for cover. The large tree trunk legs attempted to steady themselves, but the nerves would no longer respond. The legs buckled in their joints and the scorpion collapsed. And, out of feverish exhaustion, so did Ra'id.

*   *   *   *

Chapter 5

"Here is one of the... humans," said a disgusted voice. Yavin woke up immediately, but remained completely motionless,

This might the prison King Crenar keeps his captives, assumed Yavin immediately. He opened his eyes slightly so he could see the talking beings. His head thumped from exhaustion. He suddenly recalled what had happened the day before, because his hand tingled with energy.

"Are you sure it's still alive?" Said another voice. Out from the open hallway, shadows were cast against the wall. It showed two silhouettes conversing with each other. The cell Yavin was resting in was completely stone, which pained his back. But what hurt the most was his head. It felt as if it was being pounded. An abrupt thump would bump Yavin's head every so often. His skull soon began to feel as if it was going to split open.

Yavin continuously listened to the conversation between the two beings, occasionally hearing, 'Power Orb,' or 'fight to come,' and even 'The Crenarians are ready.' Eventually, one crept into the room. It had long, limber legs, brown material on its feet, which looked like shoes of some sort, and a green coloured garment made of fine silk. The figure continued to approach him cautiously, as if Yavin was toxic. Yavin closed his eyes and prepared to receive his fate.

Little does it know…it will be in for a shocking surprise, planned Yavin, who waited to spring his trap. The figure reached down, and touched him. Yavin automatically sent a small jolt of electricity through the being's body.

Now! Thought Yavin, as he sprung up and paralyzed it with his sneak attack.

Suddenly, a purple mass of a transparent fluid appeared. It absorbed the shock, which danced around in the substance, until it died away. The being was unharmed.

"Darn it! I guess I'll have to do it the hard way!" Exclaimed Yavin. He held his hands together to contain the power of the strong jolt of energy he had sent to the being before him. Energy coursed through Yavin's entire body and jumped to the being's as electricity. The body fell limp, paralyzed.

"Now where are the others?" Yavin asked himself and he sped through the stone hallways. Torches were hung along the stone hallways, casting a dim light. As he rounded the corner, he met up with two guards, except this time they had blue armour on, as opposed to the orange armour of the previous guards. They held long javelins at the ready, and carried metallic orange coloured shields.

"Hey, one of the chosen is escaping! Charge!" Ordered a deep voice under a helmet to the other.

"Sorry, but I have to do this," Yavin spoke quickly, and he coursed electricity through their bodies and moved them aside. They flailed their arms uselessly. Then, he pinned them to the wall with a current of electromagnetism.

"That should hold them for a while," murmured Yavin to himself as he sped past them. They yelled, but the cries were far behind him by then.

*   *   *   *

Down in another chamber, Ra'id had awoken to the sound of electricity crackling through the air.

"Yavin must be here!" Exclaimed Ra'id, as he got up from the stone floor and headed through the doorway. A Blavarian quickly ran to his cell and blocked the entrance.

"Halt! You're one of the chosen ones and must stay! Your powers are needed for the better of the people ~" Ra'id interrupted,

"And how do I know that you're not under King Crenar's order? Also, another question; can you swim?" Instantly, Ra'id focused his emotions to shoot water at the creature. Instead, a jet of flames careened from his hands and singed the creature's eyebrows.

"Good enough for me!" Said Ra'id to himself as he forced the air into a cushion of air for him, "Yavin! Where are you?" Whispered Ra'id down the hallway.

*   *   *   *

"Ra'id! Yavin! Tala! Where are you guys?" Sasha half whispered and shouted at the same time. She was walking along both walls, invisible, with her legs spread out. Whatever walked below her wouldn't even find her hiding spot. If someone was to come by, she'd walk up to the ceiling and stay there until it would pass.

"The inhabitants of this planet are weird. Their eyes are facing inwards, they only have three fingers and toes, and some of them even have marks on their forehead!" She said to herself. The thought of them sent shivers down her spine. She thought back of what happened with her first encounter with these beings,

Sasha's back suffered excruciating pain on the stone floor. On the ground, invisible, and waiting for a response, Sasha remained immobile. A being walked in most suddenly, looking for her. It walked over her invisible body, and as it did so, she extended her foot and tripped it. She then made a mad dash for the entrance and escaped. The creature had no clue whatsoever what had happened.

"These guys sure are strange," Sasha heard a roar echo through the halls, breaking her focus.

Down in Tala's chamber, a rampart lion was attacking several guards. They cowered behind their weapons, which were long scimitars made of a blue mineral. Seven guards lay in a corner of the room, unconscious. Tala had knocked them unconscious with a simple swipe from her enormous paw. Once swipe from the lion's claws could finish them all, but Tala stayed on her guard. She had learned the weapons were strong the hard way.

These weapons are strong. Now, let's see if they can fight fire with fire, thought Tala, as she extracted her claws.

Out came blade-like claws made of the same blue mineral. She swiped once and cut all of the blades right out of the pommel. The guards stayed there, awestruck, gazing at the weapon's handle. Then, with a ferocious roar, she sent the guards fleeing for their lives. They scurried out the door

"That should handle them for a while," said Tala with satisfaction. She transformed back to human. Energy was sapped from her body, but she still had plenty left to continue on. The roar attracted Sasha's attention, as she hurried down the hallway and found Tala.

"There you are! I've been looking for you!" Exclaimed Sasha, and the two friends hugged each other as a greeting. Then, hundreds of hot needles pierced Sasha's calf,

"Awgh!" Yelped Sasha who she fell down to the ground clenching her hand.

"What's wrong?" Asked Tala and she bent down to help her companion.

"My leg… The scorpion must've hit it," answered Sasha, and she got up slowly from the ground.

"We'd better find the other two, before they get into tr~" squeaked Tala, but she was interrupted by a loud crash of two guards, and electricity flying through the air. They also heard rocks being thrown across the room.

"Trouble. C'mon, they're bound to do something wrong." Finished Sasha and they ran into the hallway.

*   *   *   *

A laser beam streamed passed Ra'id's face, causing a tingling feeling of pure energy. He was in big trouble now. He had run into a pair of guards who were waiting for him to pass by. Thinking he could out do them, he buzzed by them, teasing them and, therefore, awakening them. But these weren't any normal guards. They had yellow armour. They had wheels. Their guns were where arms were supposed to be. They were robots. Once Ra'id had hit them with the rocks, his doom was sealed. Red lights flickered from behind the visors. It lifted its arm and fired.

This is going to be ha- Ra'id's thoughts were interrupted by another stream of light.

This time it singed his pants. He stopped concentrating on the wall and looked at his leg. There was a hole in his left pant-leg and a thin wisp of smoke escaped from it. Something gnawed at the back of his mind, trying to remind him of something.

The wisp of smoke reminded him of something. He could control fire, meaning he controlled heat.

"I'll just stop these guys cold," said Ra'id. He tapped into his powers. His brain quickly began concentrating the energy. Within seconds, he took control of the heat in the hall.

He couldn't feel much difference at first. But as he inhaled, the robots wheels creaked, but when he exhaled, they drew closer. He noticed this pattern well. Before he could inhale, the robots shot twin bullets.

Ra'id could see his life flashing before his eyes as the bullets approached. He could see and count each full revolution the bullets made as they came closer to seal his doom. He could feel the blood leave his face. His energy seemed to have vanished, and he had little strength left to move. It was when Ra'id noticed that part of his brain, the part that hadn't been used for over three thousand years by humans, was starting to spark its neurons to get moving that Ra'id's emotions were released.

The little humidity present in the room travelled faster the bullets and cocooned the bullets. The water droplets clumped together on the surface of the bullet. They quickly froze under Ra'id's control. The bullets lost their path with the added weight and hit the ground with a shattering crackle.

He exhaled, relieved. No, he wasn't free of burdens, but he would live to see another day. That was the time that Ra'id's view of life changed. He learned that every moment that he lived was a precious moment, and that he should take advantage of it.

*   *   *   *

"Sir! There's a breech in the Store room!" Yelled one of the creatures. This one had an engraving on its head, looking like a spiral. His skin was a deep tone, similar to Yavin's. His eyes seemed vaguely familiar, along with three fingers and three toes. His garments were somewhat odd. He had a black suit, and across it was an orange strip. On it were different coloured bits of stones. His build was tall and thin, and his voice sounded like a young adolescent.

"Yes, Lemmor, go on," responded a deep voice from behind the tall, leather seat.

"I think something has entered the chamber!"

"WHAT?!" Exclaimed the other being, totally surprised, "Sound the alarm," he hollered. He stood up from his seat, and he hulked over to a large chart on the wall. He looked just like the other one, but on his head was an engraving of a cross. He also had many more stones on his orange strip. The other being headed for a large, handle in the wall. He pulled it back, and released it. It flung straight into the wall again. Suddenly, a siren started sounding, and the hallways all lit up in a flashing blue light.

"That's my queue to get out of here!" Exclaimed Yavin, who stopped peering through a thin slit in the stone walls. He ran out of the hallways and into the nearest empty room.

"Good thing it's empty in here. Now I'll just wait until the alarm stops." But Yavin had no time to relax. A thick slab of steel dropped from the top of the entrance, shutting the room.

"It's not going to be that easy to keep me in here," murmured Yavin. He sent an extremely hot bolt of electricity at it. The grey door superheated. A hole melted away, and revealing the hallway once again. A wave of exhaustion flew over Yavin,

"Phew, that's tiring. Next time, maybe I should put a hold on my explosions of electricity."

But, his muttering was stopped by the sound of his friends,

"Yavin! Ra'id! Come here! Where are you?" Yavin's spirit enlightened and he found new energy to run through the hallways at full speed. He rounded the bend, and ran into Tala and Sasha,

"Finally, there you are bro!" Squeaked tiny Tala. She cleared the dust from her shirt and helped him up.

"Now we have to go find Ra'id," Yavin said. Suddenly, but with perfect timing, a huge hole formed in a wall close by. And from it emerged Ra'id,

"There you all are! It took me a while to dig through this whole maze." He joined the group and they travelled together through the whole convention of stone mazes, not knowing what lay ahead.

*   *   *   *

After about an hour of walking, they finally reached a large brass wall, which had strange symbols painted on it. One of them was five dots; another was a wisp of smoke. One was an array of dots all around one circle. The fourth was just an array of dots. Then the last two were the same two symbols that Yavin saw earlier, the cross and the spiral.

"These symbols seem… familiar, as if in a different life I saw them before…" remarked Ra'id, and he started to reach over to touch one,

"What did you say?" asked Tala. Her ears continuously rang to the sound of the alarm though it had stopped fifteen minutes ago.

"I don't think you should touch~" started Sasha, but Ra'id had already done so. The wall creaked and moaned. The six symbols illuminated, giving off a purple aura. Sasha whispered to her companions,

"What did you do?" The door suddenly gave into the magical force that pulled aside the two rusty pieces. The slabs creaked and moaned, as if they hadn't been opened for so long.

On the other side of the door was a vast hallway. In it were dusty rocks, and at the center lay two floating spheres. One was a larger blue ball, and it made the children feel strange. As if they were being rocketed down a rollercoaster when it came to a free fall. Their stomachs turned upside down when they saw it. But they didn't know what it was. They all pondered this feeling. Then, when their eyes fell on the smaller purple one, they felt normal again.

Yavin broke the silence,

"Well, now we know what was on the other side of the door."

"What's that blue ball? It made me feel... new," They walked further into the room. Tala found that the ruins weren't actually rocks, but were actually pillars naturally erected from the ground. The ground was covered with a centimetre of dust,

"When was the last time someone came in here?" Yavin asked as he brushed his finger against the smooth pillar surfaces. His finger came up all covered in grey soot. Sasha answered his question,

"Maybe they couldn't come in here. Maybe it could only be opened by people destined to open it..."

"I think I know who might be able to open too. Maybe it has to do with those symbols," suggested Ra'id. He searched through the rubble for treasures. His curiosity urged him on, and he had made it halfway across the hall.

"That reminds me of those things I saw," remembered Yavin. He recalled the time he was eavesdropping, "Two of these creatures were in the room. One had a spiral engraved on his head, like that one on the door. The other had a cross engraved on his forehead."

Ra'id finally stopped feeling the lure pulling him across the hall and he looked down at the ground. Within the rubble, a glint of light shined from underneath. He reached down, but couldn't reach it while he floated,

Maybe I'll just stop hovering for two seconds and move away some rubble and dirt. With quick movements, Ra'id descended to the sharp rocks. Then he leaped off the cushion of air and onto the ground. When he touched it, something strange happened.

Ra'id was lifted from the ground. Ra'id looked up to the blue ball. It pulsed happily, cheery to see its old friend back. A sudden blue wave of energy and light flew across the hallway. The four children felt the wave drift into each one of them, energy spiralling haphazardly within it.

"My... My arm. It's completely healed. That strange ball must have something to do with it. It sent a wave of power through me as if it knows-" Sasha was saying,

"Who we are," finished Ra'id.

He leaned down and removed the rubble from the glittering object. As the dust cleared, he reached for the mystifying alloy that glinted to an invisible ray of light. His hand grasped it perfectly, and he soon found out it was a handle made of an orange mineral. He pulled his arm back with a strenuous heave. The handle came up from the ground along with a wooden plank. Underneath was a winding tunnel, spiralling into the depths of Xecwer.

"Hey, guys! I found a secret passage of some sort. Maybe it'll lead us out of this huge fortress. Maybe, just maybe, it'll lead us to Raghouik," beckoned Ra'id. The friends hesitated. The last time they listened to him, they ended up in a dark alley with Raghouik breathing down their necks.

*　　*　　*　　*

The tunnel was pretty dark. It was wide and high, so the companions weren't crunched together. But a small drizzle flowed on the stone floor, leaving a long trail of green mould along the side. They had been walking for half an hour, and already they were getting tired. Some rats had run down the tunnel and back, fighting for the remainders of their kin. They continued a little more, hoping the tunnel had an end. A half hour later, Yavin broke the silence,

"Great. A dead end. We've got to turn back before the guards find the passage way and trap us in here."

"No. I'm picking up vibrations." Tala moved her hand around the wall in the darkness. Ra'id could sense something different in the earth. Something that was stirring. There was something on the other side of the wall. Tala reached over and felt a handprint. Her hand slid neatly into it. The indent lit up in a bright orange. The same orange spread out within the wall, and large orange veins lit up, like water filling a convention of tunnels. The wall disintegrated where the orange veins were, and the wall's support was lost. It collapsed, forming an entrance to a vast hallway.

Sunlight beamed down from a hole in the ceiling and landed a the dusty red ground.

"A way out! Yes! Sweet fresh air at last!" Sasha exclaimed and she rushed past the pile of rubble. She ran everywhere, happy to be free. She abruptly stopped when she heard a sudden crunch under her feet.

She glanced down on what she had stepped on. Sasha lifted her foot and saw shattered, pieces of something hard on the outside and soft in the middle. Marrow was oozing slowly from it. She then looked on what were only centimetres away from her foot. It looked like a curved cage of a thin white material. She looked further from the cage and saw a skull. It seemed to be grinning at her, its eyes casting a sinister look. She was standing on a skeleton,

"Eek! A skeleton! Get it away from me!" Squealed Sasha and she hurried over to her left. She heard another crunch,

"Another skeleton!" Sasha looked around to see hundreds of skeletons lying on the ground, and gasped. Some had three pairs of eyes. Others had four arms. Some were on four legs. Some had weapons, and others didn't. And all of them looked as if they had turned their heads towards Sasha, grinning at her disturbance. What was worse was that something seemed to be alive in this prison of frozen skeletons. Something that was aware of their presence. Sasha scurried back to the entrance and stayed there.

The others slowly walked into the field. The heads seemed to gaze at their latest living intruders. Some of the skeletons stood there, covering their eyes. Some crouched, and some kneeled with fright. Ra'id broke the solemn silence,

"It's impossible for these skeleton's keep their positions like this. Unless they were~" he was interrupted by Yavin,

"Killed with magic or a dangerous power,"

"Maybe so," said Ra'id, and he examined the weapons that were scattered amongst them. One was a gun, of sorts, with a compartment the size of a baseball. It was blue, glistening even in the shadows. A glass window showed a small capsule the size of Ra'id's thumb. But inside, Ra'id could see… things, writhing lively, waiting to be released. He shuddered and looked away.

The most human like weapon was probably a scimitar, but it was made from a blue metal. Ra'id searched through the armaments for a weapon. After much rummaging, a gauntlet had aroused his curiosity. It was made of an orange metal, adorned with lively patterns. He pulled it off of the hand of the creature's skeleton. The glove had five fingers. He slipped it on, thinking it would be a nice token of good luck. However, it was several sizes larger than his hand.

Suddenly, a hum filled the air. The glove began to glow, like the ball had. It almost was pulsating a rhythmic beat, as if it, too, were alive. Then it came to life. The fingers of the glove contracted, forcing Ra'id's hand to follow in suit. The metal dug into Ra'id's skin as the metal shifted in his palm. The gauntlet grew tighter around him. When the light dissimulated, it had adjusted to his hand, fitting perfectly. He admired it, seeing dancing circles rolling on his palm.

"Ra'id, you've been standing there for a while. What's the matter? The skeleton's scaring you?" Yavin teased, and he hurried over to him.

"What Yavin? What do you want? I was just admiring some of these weapons. This planet's got quite an arsenal," responded Ra'id, who continued, this time speaking to all of his companions, "Shouldn't we take a weapon to defend ourselves better against the people of this planet? We shouldn't waste our energy by using our powers. We should take a weapon." Sasha gave her opinion,

"We don't even know how to use these weapons. We might as well keep our normal powers. We can absorb energy all over here." Tala agreed,

"These weapons are also heavy. We'll slow down with them."

"Fine. You guys can be weapon less, while I'll use," Ra'id looked for a weapon, trying to find something worth fighting with. "Aha! This scimitar is swift and easy to use."

He lifted it off from the ground. Suddenly, a force seemed to take control of him. His head started aching. He went dizzy as he felt himself being pulled away from his body. A strange force had taken hold of him, and Ra'id's conscious didn't stand a chance against its shear force. He twirled the sword, swivelled it, and spun around and pretended to sword fight. He parried with inhuman speed and lunged several times within the same second.

"Ra'id! Where did you learn how to swordfight! I never knew you could. Maybe you could teach us," exclaimed Yavin.

I didn't know I could either! Thought Ra'id, not knowing what he was meddling with,

"Why don't you guys choose a weapon? Some of these are easy to use. Such as… this bow! Yavin, take this bow here. As for arrows…" The gauntlet jerked in his hand and forced his left arm to rise. The earth shook from beneath him, though Ra'id had barely tweaked his emotions. A skeleton leaped to life, controlled by Ra'id, or so it seemed. The twig-like ribs snapped off and straightened out. They resembled thin sticks. Ra'id's earth senses were knocked on, something he had never done before. A strange feeling came over him as his senses prodded through the soil, searching for something. A tingly feeling filled him. The ground split, and chunks of metal shot out from the ground. He removed it from the ground, forged them into crude arrowheads, and fused them to the shafts with his heat energy.

Ra'id's conscious came back to his body. He could move freely again, and he could think for himself.

"Wow. I… didn't know I could do that. I guess these arrows will do for now. Now, Tala, I think these purple things might be useful," pointed Ra'id feebly, and he took the purple blobs with blue netting around it. There were about fifteen scattered around the chamber, strapped to belts of the skeletons.

"Sasha… if you don't want a weapon, you don't need one," Ra'id said. Sasha replied,

"Good. I don't want to join your guerrilla warfare, or whatever it is. I'll just fight with my powers."

"Suit yourself. We better get out of here before the guards find us," implied Ra'id. The gauntlet on his left hand began to glow, leaving streaks against the wall behind him.

"Umm… Ra'id. What's that behind you?" Asked Yavin and he came closer.

"Nothing, nothing at all. Why do you ask?" Answered Ra'id, who was trying to dig the glove into his shirt,

"Ra'id, a light is shining from behind. Show us!" Demanded Tala. Ra'id finally took his hand from behind his back and showed them the gauntlet. It's blue and green patterns were shining brightly, flowing along his forearm.

"It's a gauntlet I had found earlier on a skeleton's hand. I'm sorry I didn't tell you guys earlier," answered Ra'id, and he dropped his head. He, however, did not reveal the fact that it was… alive.

"It doesn't matter. It's your 'weapon', I suppose." The gauntlet continued shining, and then finally, the blue and green patterns turned into visible words, but in a different language. He blinked once, then twice and the letters formed words. He read it out loud,

"'Do not make haste, yet no time to waste, beware and befriend those at the sunlight's end.' It must be some kind of paradox. We shouldn't hurry, but there's no time to waste. 'Beware and befriend?' What's that mean? Those at sunlight's end…" They all turned towards the tip where the sunlight reached from the open space in the wall, and saw no one.

Ra'id's air senses started to pick a different scent. One that hadn't appeared until more recently. Some might say that it was the smell of 'fear'. Or, less commonly known as adrenaline. Either way, someone or something had quickly begun to panic. The other children followed Ra'id's gaze when the heard a slippery voice declare,

"Leinad, I think we've found the chosen ones…"

Chapter 6

"Well done, Sa'rin, now the chosen ones will follow us to the~" the creature called Leinad stepped into the sunlight, but was interrupted by Yavin,

"We won't follow you! You'll follow us!" He sent a jolt of lightening to the two creatures. A glow grew from the two of them. Their particles were torn apart before the electricity could reach them. They assimilated several feet away. Leinad's forehead was glowing. It dimmed and revealed an engraving on it, which looked like an array of dots, similar to the one on the big, rusty doors,

"We are both friends of you. We oppose the King Crenar, and are in need of your help and leadership. Will you join us?" Leinad asked and both of them bowed down, kneeling on their right knees. Leinad's hair was black and wild, while the other had straight brown hair at shoulder height. Sasha noticed that Leinad had three fingers, like the other creatures, but Sa'rin had five, like a human. Sa'rin's icy eyes weren't at an angle at all, but a chill creped down Sasha's spine when she looked at her.

"We would be honoured to lead your organization and rebel against King Crenar," said Ra'id, and he held up his right hand. The two beings got up from the ground and bowed again. Leinad wore a green vest, with a band across it, and the other being wore the same, but its vest was blue. The pants were patched up with different kinds of materials, and the shoes were soft, and made of cloth. Leinad looked young, several years over Ra'id's age, while the other looked older. Leinad beckoned them to follow, and they entered a tunnel. He began to speak, in a young inquisitive voice,

"It looks like you already have found weapons. Very good. After we tour you around this whole fortress, you can begin to train in battle with your weapons. The time soon falls to plan a rebellion against the King. Right now, I'll take you to the Blavarial community."

They continued to walk in darkness. Ra'id decided to light up the tunnel with fire. With his left hand raised, he snapped his fingers and created a single flame,

"Ooh, amazing! It also appears that you have already learned to control your powers," exclaimed Leinad happily, unable to contain his enthusiasm. The flame continued to flicker, and the companions continued on. When they came to an end, Sa'rin in her sly, snake-like voice,

"Now, we are about to meet the public, waiting for you. Look like born leaders by straightening yourselves," at this point she slapped Yavin in the back to straighten him, "and lifting your hands in the air. In the middle of the parade, you will be asked to show your powers. Show them in every which way that you can."

The door opened, and there stood a crowd of thousands. Brilliant lights flashed and shined everywhere. Some people wore old clothes; others wore dazzling clothes. Their eyes all faced slightly inwards, and some even waved their three fingered hands. Some held coloured banners. Screams were heard across the hall. The ceiling was of rock, and the ground was carpeted. The place seemed like a giant parade, but inside a cavern.

"Where exactly are we?" Sasha asked, noticing the cave.

"We're in a valley, hidden underground. It's the only place Crenar hasn't reached or found." Ra'id simply shrugged at

Leinad's response and carried on. The companions walked along a platform. They sat down on seats made of the same orange metal. Silence fell upon the crowd as Leinad took the front,

"Fellow Blavarians, I have ill and good tidings to bring. Raghouik, our past leader, has been captured by Crenar," gasps were heard from the crowd when the name was said. Some shuddered, and a baby started to whine. A chill crept down Tala's neck though the air was humid and sticky,

"So I will take his place as Vice-president and Head Connoisseur. The good news is this; the Catalysts have been found and have agreed to govern over my command. Let the parade begin!" He took a seat, and a buzzing sound filled the air. It was high pitched, and it filled the ears of everyone. The sound began to drop, and then drums gonged and filled the hall with noise. The crowd began shouting again. Suddenly, the platform the thrones were standing on began to move, and it slowly advanced across the great hall.

Two hours into the parade, the companions were getting tired of waving. Tala had almost fallen asleep, but Yavin had awoken before anyone could notice. Then, Leinad roused his companions,

"Now is the time to show your abilities. We'll start with you," and he pointed to Tala,

"Do what you do best…" He didn't exactly know what their abilities were.

"What's your name, anyway?"

Tala seemed to glance away, gave a questioning glance at her brother, who nodded, then stuttered,

"T – Tala,"

"Now you," he then pointed to Yavin,

Leinad continued asking the same questions. Once he finished with Ra'id, he said to the people,

"Now, the chosen ones will show you their powers, and will amaze you with a dazzling show" He left the stage to present Tala, who got from her seat. He said,

"I give you, Tala!"

She wanted to impress the crowd. She thought deeply into her imagination for the feelings of a phoenix, made sure she knew, and ran off the platform. The crowd gasped in awe. The moment she was off the ground, she started shrinking. Red-orange feathers sprouted from her arms. Her legs shrank further, and yellow scales grew. Feathers covered her whole body. A beak protruded from her mouth. Three long purple stalks came from the back of her neck, and curled at the top. She finished her transformation flew gracefully. She looped over. The crowd 'Oohed' and 'Aahed', and she landed back on the platform. She transformed back to human and took a swift, confident bow.

"Bravo! Bravo!" Whistles were heard from the crowd amidst the applause.

"Here is Yavin!" Yavin jumped from his seat and began. He quickly focused his energy into orange electricity. Spheres of electricity crackled in his hands as he began to juggle three or four of them. The speed picked up within seconds. Eventually, Yavin's arms were but a blur. The spheres moved so fast that all you could see was an orange loop coming from Yavin's hands. However, he lost control and each one was sent through the ceiling. Cleanly burnt holes could be seen there, with sunlight flooding the hall.

Leinad ignored it and continued,

"Next up is Sasha!" Sasha stood up and came to the front. She loosened her shoulders, and stretched. She quickly vanished. The crowd grew silent. She stretched her arms, and reached for a banner someone was holding. The expression on the face of the creature was puzzled. The crowd didn't notice much at all. Sasha laughed coolly, and left the banner. She turned visible and brought back her arms. The group all laughed in unison.

"Very nice. Now, for the last of them all, here is Ra'id." Ra'id walked to the front, and lifted his hands, and made two over-sized droplets in each. He tossed them in the air calmly. The crowd followed them as they began to fall. Ra'id quickly tossed a fire ball at it, producing a bit of smoke. With a twirl of his arms, he whipped up a cyclone, which quickly broke from his control and dashed across the hall. He winced as it narrowly missed a pedestrian.

Ra'id suddenly began feeling pulled away. His conscious was all he had control of. He could feel himself performing. Except his wasn't controlling the performance. It was something much more. Ra'id felt himself covering his right leg with rock, his left with water, his right clutching a fireball and his left hand containing a tornado. He never felt like this before. This powerful. He lost focus, and the elements ran amuck with the chamber. The tornado caught fire and spiralled haphazardly within the chamber. Ra'id remembered where he was and quickly doused it with the earth and water.

He let out an embarrassed bow over all of the commotion and sheepishly returned to his seat.

Ra'id felt different. Drowsy, fatigued, and dizzy. It was when the room went fuzzy that he realized that he was fainting. Not that he was panicking, or anything. It was just that he had very little energy left to go on. He closed his eyes and relaxed.

*   *   *   *

"Revnos!" That was the word Ra'id woke to. The word itself set a fire in his stomach, and energy started flowing through him. He opened his eyes to see a soft, purple glow, and three fingers encasing it. The light was pulled away, to reveal a curious face. It had an engraving on its head; a wisp of smoke. Its hair was black and curled, with a slightly tanned skin. Its ears were curved back at the top a bit.

"Ahwg, my head," Ra'id got up from the bed, and rubbed his head. The creature got up from the bed and walked away. Ra'id got up and looked around. It was another grey, stone room. After a couple of minutes, Leinad walked in,

"Ra'id! You've finally awakened." Thousands of questions flew through Ra'id's mind; his mouth was unable to contain them,

"How long have I've slept?"

"It's been about two hours,"

"Two hours?! What happened? Why did I pass out?!"

"The Gauntlet of Blavarix. That's what happened. That gauntlet you wear, a thing of the devil… manipulates whatever it holds. It uses maximum energy. It was a weapon, designed by Blavarix himself."

"What? What are you talking about?"

"Blavarix is the founder of this rebellion. The name 'Blavarian' was derived from his name."

"I know it means that! And what about this metal glove?" Ra'id held up his left hand and pointed at it.

"That gauntlet was made of one of the rarest metal of the entire planet; Xecweranite. It has the ability to contain ether; energy waiting to be Catalyzed. Then, he fused powers of the Power Orb to the gauntlet. Whatever was held in the rings of that palm," Leinad pointed at the blue circles in the palm of the gauntlet, and he continued, "Could be controlled by the power of the owner. For instance, if you held a rock in your hand, you could easily turn it into water, or even fire, and you could turn it back. A wise man taught Blavarix how to blacksmith the finest crafts, because he foresaw a great future in him. But now," Leinad's voice dropped, "After Blavarix's apprenticism, the trainer left to travel the world and never returned. They say he was captured and thrown into the Prison of Gillautinixe,"

"What prison?"

"Gillautinixe is the city where Crenar resides. In the prison, the prisoners are left in rooms where the walls blind them. At night, demons enter the chambers to steal energy from the captives. I don't know if he's still alive, but if he is, he's on the brink of death.

"The last time we saw him was when his opaque body was carried away slowly.

Leinad placed his hand on the door, and it opened slowly. It creaked and groaned, but gave away finally. Ra'id entered the room. The two orbs floated gloomily at the center of the room. Leinad spoke up,

"The blue one is the Power Orb. That is the source of your powers. The purple one is the Traits Orb. It's the reason for this engraving on my head," Leinad pointed at his head, "It grants me a defence, whenever danger strikes." Ra'id was about to speak, but Leinad continued, "The reason why I brought you here is because of that gauntlet. When the magic was fused to that gauntlet, the excess energy was left alone. Suddenly, it fused into the Traits Orb. Six Xecwerians were granted its power. However, Blavarix overlooked one law of magical artefacts; each ingredient must be precise. In doing so, your glove was..." Leinad trailed off. Suddenly, Ra'id noticed that Leinad couldn't look straight into Ra'id's eyes, nor at the gauntlet,

"What's with this gauntlet?" Leinad suddenly noticed he'd stopped talking. He hesitated, then quickly added,

"Never mind."

Chapter 7

Ra'id ran quickly through the vast hallway, sidestepping rubble that was in his way. After what seem like a long run, he reached the end of the room. There were drawings on the wall but he didn't recall any of them. They depicted stick-men with swords and shields, all chasing one person in the middle. This person was larger, and his hands glowed blue. Ra'id continued to observe, but one stick figure with a scimitar caught his eye. His weapon had stabbed one figure in the middle. The hand with the scimitar was covered by a gauntlet. Blavarix's gauntlet! He reached over to feel the wall. Suddenly, a bright orange light lit the entire wall - except for a rectangular spot. Ra'id hurried over to it and examined the spot. Nothing seemed different. He felt the wall, and his hand was able to penetrate it as if it was not there,

"Whoa! Must be some kind of illusion!" He walked right through the wall, and found his friends on the other side.

"It's about time you got here. I am known as Lemmor," said a tall, young Xecwerian. He was standing in a green field. He had almost no hair, and had an orange strip, like a sash, across his chest. The engraving on his head was a spiral.

I know him. He was the one talking to the general, recalled Yavin, searching deep within his thoughts.

He wore a black suit, and along the orange strip were several kinds of stones of many colours. The one beside him was a bit taller. He wore the same garments, but his strip had many more stones and his forehead was marked with a cross. This one had wild brown-blond hair that curled slightly.

"Here, beside me," continued Lemmor,

"Is Se'maj. He's the General," the being named Se'maj took a bow, and Lemmor continued,

"The next one is Gir'heg." This Xecwerian wore a simple light blue robe, and green pants. His engraving was a wisp of smoke, just like the one on the large doors. He wore a thick black belt. Purple spheres surrounded in blue netting were strapped along it.

"He's our ranger. You two," and he pointed to Yavin and Tala,

"Will learn from him.

"Your next instructor is Ne'hoj," he gestured towards one with a scope closed on his eye, attached to his ear. A strap across his chest had many small cylinders. His forehead had an engraving of an array of dots surrounding one circle. He was leaning on a large gun. You wouldn't've wanted to cross him in a dark alleyway. His garments were a mix of deep green and black camouflage, and he had dirt-blond hair.

"And he's our assassin. His assistant has a keen sense of things around here, Na'yr," he pointed to the one beside Ne'hoj. He had shades on, with an engraving of five dots. His hair was also dirt blonde. He had a scythe of which he leaned on, and wore the same clothes as Ne'hoj.

"These two need to be quick and sharp if they're to be assassins, so they'll teach you, Sasha,"

"I'm the supervisor, Se'maj will be setting some obstacle courses, and Leinad will be working with you," and he pointed to Ra'id,

"Wherever he may be." Finished Lemmor. Suddenly, a brilliant light illuminated Lemmor, and Leinad appeared out of thin air.

His forehead shined, until it dimmed to a glow, to reveal the array of dots on his forehead gleaming.

"Everybody except for Sasha has been designated a weapon," Out of Leinad's palm appeared a long shaft, with blades at both ends,

"Now, all go to your stations, because there is a lot to learn and so little time," said Leinad, and walked towards Ra'id. His companions followed their trainer to a different area of the field.

Down where Tala and Yavin were, Gir'heg was explaining how they can use their weapons with powers,

"Yavin, since your arrow heads are made of these metals, you can store electricity inside the tip. Then, when the arrow is released, the tip will send a jolt of electricity to the target. I suggest you infuse your arrows now. Here's how you do it," he reached for one of Yavin's arrows. Then, he held it to Yavin,

"You must hold the tip. Then, heat your hand with electricity, but not to hot," Yavin grasped the tip of the arrow and waited for further instructions,

"Then, focus on the electricity coursing through the arrow, but don't focus on the electricity in your hand." Yavin concentrated hard, and let energy flow from him to the arrow. After he dispensed some of his energy, he stopped, and opened his palm. There lay the arrow tip's orange metal infused into a bright orange blob.

"You overheated it," Gir'heg said with a tone of chicanery, and continued,

"Here, take one of my arrows," he bent his arm behind and reached for his quiver. He took out an arrow made with a shaft of wood and a tip of blue,

"It is much cheaper, but it works just as well," but Yavin asked a question,

"What do you mean by 'Cheaper'?"

"That blue metal my arrow's have," he held another one of his arrows, and pointed towards the tip,

73

"Is a hard metal called Blavarite. It's very bountiful in this area of Blavarians. But, a more expensive kind," he tapped Yavin's other arrow,

"Is a lot harder to find, and is only used as rewards and for jewellery we sell. That metal can store more energy than Blavarite. So try it again with this cheap arrow, and don't focus too much on the hand, mainly on the arrow." Yavin did as he was told.

A small amount of energy was sapped out of him and placed into the arrow tip. When he opened his palm, the blue arrow tip had small jolts of electricity running through it, lightening escaping in all directions.

"Wow! That's awesome! I'll do it to the rest of my arrows." Yavin finished supplying his arrows with electricity one by one. They all shined in his quiver. As he put his last arrow inside, he asked,

"Is there somewhere in this Blavarial community where I can buy arrows? I need more than ten!"

"Yavin," Gir'heg answered, "All that counts with your ten arrows is how you use them. If I have one hundred in my quiver, doesn't mean I'll reach my target. Tend these arrows wisely, and they will help you," he finished, and patted Yavin on the back.

"Now Tala, you have these weapons," Gir'heg pointed to the small purple orbs she had around her waist,

"They are called Plasma nets. The liquid inside it stuns the target on contact, and the net traps them. It not much of a threat, so your powers are a lot better. The nets are used to trap foe if they threaten you," he snapped off one of them that was hanging off his chest strap, and held it towards her, "Use them wisely, because they could be the difference between life and death," Tala posed a question very shyly,

"Can I make these or maybe reuse it? Uh... I only have fifteen."

"You can. The Traits Orb lets off this purple substance. It has a natural stunning ability. If you had it carefully harvested some, you can drop it into these small nets,"

"Now, I'll have to see what your capabilities are," several targets with bull's-eyes appeared. In front of Tala a couple of rocks about the same size as the orbs appeared, and in front of Yavin, twenty arrows with stone tips.

"You shall both aim and hit the targets with these objects!" announced Gir'heg. Yavin pulled his maple bow to so that his eye and arrow were in line. He aimed for several seconds... then fired.

On the opposite side of the field, Sasha was learning how to fight with a sari'kun, a long wooden stick with sharp orange blades at the end,

"First, spread your legs as if you're riding a horse. This will keep your balance. Also, always have one foot slightly in front of the other," grunted Ne'hoj, and he pulled his legs to an arc position. Sasha did so, and held the sari'kun in front of her with both arms.

"Since you're both flexible and agile, you should be a good assassin. Now, keep the sari'kun in front of you at an angle. This is the defensive pose." Sasha struggled to keep the sari'kun in the air; it was fairly heavy.

"Now, take one of your hands, pull the staff back. Use the other to reach forward." Sasha bent the stick downwards, until it pointed straight,

"I guess this is the attack position," she said. Na'yr nodded and said,

"Now, try practicing that with these dummies. They're spring-loaded, so they will retaliate." He pointed to a couple of rag dolls suspended by sticks. Some had buttons as eyes. Were missing its head. Sasha took a deep sigh and approached one of them. She glared down on it, and swung her sari'kun to its chest.

Down at the entrance of the field, Ra'id snored on as Leinad kept talking about Blavarix,

I bet you this thing is a curse! I can't even take it off! Thought Ra'id, who tried to slip off the glove.

"… The gauntlet was used by the great Blavarix himself, and, with his ~" Leinad paused, and noticed Ra'id was fast asleep,

"Can't you see how important this is?! You'll never know the history of this foundation!" Leinad grabbed him by the shoulders and shook him awake. Ra'id let out a yawn,

"And? Do I care about the history of this place? No. Besides, this won't help me when I'm a second from dying. You can see what training I might need… with a sword fight!" Suggested Ra'id, and he cracked his knuckles and picked up his scimitar, swishing it expertly.

The same power took control again, and his conscious was squeezed to the back of his mind. Something else was in control. Something dark and evil that didn't have body, living *off* Ra'id, like a parasite.

"Fine by me, then, Mister Know-it-all! Let's see who can knock their opponent three times off their feet. And if you get hurt, don't blame me." Leinad shrugged and hurried over to Ra'id. Leinad bowed quickly, shot straight back up, and started the fight.

Ra'id commenced by swivelling his scimitar in all directions and alternating hands. It cleanly passed the other two blades on Leinad, which couldn't parry the attack. As it came closer to Leinad's heart, he swiped the sword away. Then, he formed an X out of the swords and approached Ra'id at a quick pace. Instinctively, Ra'id put the sword aligned with his body and pirouetted out of the way. Then, with a quick jolt, he smashed the pommel of his sword with the spine of Leinad. This happened so quickly, he couldn't react. He absorbed the shock and fell to the ground.

"One down, two to go," Ra'id had hissed malevolently, and he took back to his defensive stance and raised the sword across his chest. Pain continued to splinter through Leinad's back, as he slowly arose to the ground.

"Get used to it, Leinad; you're going to meet the ground a lot more." Cried Ra'id and he laughed an evil cry. Leinad looked closely and remarked what he wished he hadn't; a deep shadow flickering within Ra'id's eyes. He was being possessed, possessed by a devilish entity

Anger simmered within Leinad. He was not just about to lose to an amateur swordsman. Or was he? He quickly put the swords in front of himself and attacked aggressively. He poked at one side, and prodded at another. He skinned Ra'id's side. He held it in agony. The shadow disappeared, and Leinad knew Ra'id was himself again. He dropped his head to examine the wound, but quickly lifted it. The ghost jumped across his eyes again. He barred his teeth and advanced. Leinad back away, obviously intimidated. Ra'id counted Leinad's steps. As Leinad lifted his foot, Ra'id pulled aside the earth behind him. The gauntlet glowed, and suddenly, Leinad fell into the ditch. Two falls to nothing, Ra'id's favour, and Leinad was exhausted. He climbed out, and kneeled to regain some energy.

As unsportsmanlike it might have seemed, the gauntlet jumped to life and focused a ball of compressed air in its host's hand. A vacuum started within it, and it spiralled into a cyclone. Once the pressure was high enough, the gauntlet released it. It swayed from side to side as it hurried over to Leinad. He lifted his head, wondering what the noise was, and saw the cyclone about to collide with him head on. Ra'id tasted sweet victory in his mouth. But this quickly ended. The symbol on Leinad's forehead glowed, and he disappeared. The cyclone shredded through nothing, and stopped.

A bright ball appeared behind Ra'id. He noticed the light and turned. Out of it jumped Leinad. He slammed his swords' pommels against Ra'id's chest, and sent him straight to the ground.

"You might learn a thing or two at these training grounds, eh, Ra'id," taunted Leinad, and he leaned against one of his scimitars. A creepy voice slithered through Ra'id's mind;

Show him no mercy… Show no mercy… Show him the pain… A shiver crawled up Ra'id's spine.

What are you?

Your consciousness... Do as I say... Suddenly, Ra'id was engulfed by an invisible force.

He was quickly re-possessed.

No mercy... He thought malevolently. Ra'id waited for the right moment.

When Leinad least expected it, he turned around from the ground and jumped up to hit Leinad's sword with white fire. It melded with the other scimitar, and sank into the ground. Leinad fell to the ground, stunned. The gauntlet glowed, and Ra'id showed the blade to Leinad. He prepared to deliver the final blow.

Finish him! Ra'id heard.

Chapter 8

"No!" Ra'id overtook the gauntlet and threw the blade to the ground, beside Leinad, who was sweating in fear.

Ra'id's spirit suddenly broke itself free from the congestion, his possession ending. He gasped for breath, the gauntlet gaining strength.

"S – s – sorry Leinad… I didn't – it wasn't my fault,"

"We'll see, Ra'id. This is only the beginning," Leinad lifted himself from the ground. His pant leg was torn, and blood streaked across his mouth. Anger and fear mixed in his eye. He raised his voice to speak to everyone else, "Enough training now. We shall go to the dining hall after you get changed at your rooms. Clothes will be laid on the bed for you. Attach the dagger to your belt, just in case of any~"

Suddenly, a siren sounded. A hole opened from the ceiling, and out dropped a siren. It spun and red lights filled the room.

"That's the alarm! Something's endangering the Blavarial community!" hollered Lemmor over the chaos. Yavin hit his last target in the bull's-eye. Sasha furiously slashed off the head of the dummy. The companions hurried over to hear the news,

"We need you four and your powers to stop this… creature. It's most probably a cave rat, eating the supplies. We need you to act and destroy it," Se'maj continued; "I'll take you to the storage room." He beckoned everyone to hurry up towards a tree in the field. He knocked three times. Nothing happened at once. Then steam erupted from the creases, and a door revealed itself. They entered a winding tunnel. Dust polluted the air, and oozed crept across the floor,

"This secret passage hasn't been revealed to anyone – not even Sar'in, the Chief Advisor. Hurry now, through the passage." Se'maj ushered them quickly, as they squeezed through a thin channel.

A couple of minutes had passed, and crawling was the only thing happening. Tala trudged through the tunnel wearily. Something rubbed against her leg. It frightened her, causing her to stumble. She fell into the wall where Se'maj had stopped. He quickly pushed the wall aside, revealing a new room.

When the dust had settled, Tala lifted her head. She could here screeches and wings beating behind her. Everybody hurried out of the cave. Then they saw it. The Xecwerians were surprised to see it. It was the legendary Batorat. It was a giant rat, about three feet tall. It had curved scythe-like claws, and eyes with blazing retinas. The end of the tail was unusual. It had a club with spikes. But the most unusual characteristics were its ears and shoulders. Its ears were a foot high each. A thin membrane had replaced the cartilage, making the arteries visible. And on its shoulders were long scarlet wings. It had a wingspan of at least ten meters.

Sasha let out a blood curdling scream. It heard her well. It stopped feasting on its meal (Xecweranite) and turned its head. The fiery eyes focused on the group. As if it were searching their souls, it stared deeply into pair of eyes.

"This is going to be harder than I thought," explained Se'maj, while Na'yr tried to calm Sasha down. Se'maj's inward eyes became crossed and filled with courage, "This creature was only existed in a legend. The only person who had ever found one was Crenar... I have no clue whatsoever how it got here. It is said to be able to spew flames, capable of causing large gales, and shredding any substance with its claws. It'll be hard to defeat, because this is no normal beast. Its legendary appeal is not just those reasons; it can read minds and understand Xecwerian. It will know what we're plotting, so it'll be hard to beat it. Any ideas?" Se'maj shrugged to everyone. The Batorat became impatient. It snorted, and flames spewed out like a stream.

It eyes glowed brightly. It focused on the group in front it. They started to sweat profusely because the heat had skyrocketed. They almost fainted before Lemmor broke the silence,

"The Batorat has heat vision! We'll have to include that in the chronicles," said Lemmor, and he pulled out a notepad and jotted some notes down.

"Lemmor! You're writing notes while the Batorat is going to singe us to ashes!" complained Sasha. Very coincidently, Lemmor passed out, the heat too much for him.

All of the companions heard a hiss in their thoughts, 'One down.'

"We've got to do something else," exclaimed Na'yr, "Sasha, hoist Leinad up to the Batorat. Leinad, have your sword. Ra'id, keep us safe from the fire,"

"Got it,"

"Tala, transform into a phoenix, annoy the beast, and try to get it flying,"

"Yavin," he looked over his shoulder,

"I know what needs to be done," Na'yr saluted everyone good luck. He hurried to the corner with Se'maj, who was healing Lemmor.

Sasha kept her arms stiff and very carefully stretched them. Tala quickly transformed into the phoenix. She soared through the air. But she no match compared to the Batorat. The Batorat flapped its wings, creating a gale. It might have been a gale for it, but not Tala. She fought hard to keep moving. When the Batorat tired, she streaked through the air, and started pecking at its head. The Batorat immediately swung its arms above. Tala was too quick, and she got a bit higher. The Batorat lifted off the crag it was perched upon.

Ra'id seized his chance. Tala was too slow now that the Batorat was flying. He dropped boulders onto it, and crushed its wings. The Batorat shrieked, and focused its eyes on Ra'id. It glowed again from that heat aura. But Ra'id quickly retaliated. He whipped up a cyclone around the monster. It lost its focus completely.

Yavin knew it was his turn. He moved his hands rapidly. Then, in a subtle moment, a lightning bolt struck the creature. It stopped flailing in the cyclone, dazed. Yavin sent electricity to carry it from the cyclone to Leinad. Leinad stood on a wobbly stand. Sasha was supporting him. Leinad focused. He drew his sword, and waited for his chance.

The Batorat regained consciousness, and started to thrash. Yavin couldn't control it. He released the creature, and it flew through the air. It met eyes with Leinad. It took a deep breath, and its chest expanded. A red glow filled its belly, and the room heated up. Leinad gave the signal for Sasha to let go. She tightened her arms, and Leinad jumped right in front of the Batorat. That instant, it released an eruption of flames. But the flames danced past Leinad. He was replaced with a glow, which disappeared. From behind the Batorat jumped Leinad from a void. He sliced the back of the beast's head, splitting its spine.

A cry of anguish pierced the dead silence. The body of the Batorat fell limp, and it descended to the ground. Leinad rejoiced his victory, but not for long. He gazed down to the ground to see it quickly approaching him. He soon realised that it was him that was plummeting closer to his doom. No one could help him, and they all gazed at him uselessly as his fate drew closer. When Leinad was only bare feet from the ground, he closed his eyes and awaited his fate.

Chapter 9

He expected the crunching noise of his bones squishing together. Or, he thought his life would've ended there, without too much pain. Then again, he was falling from about a hundred feet in the air. Gir'heg would be lucky not be scraping him off the rock floor. Suddenly, he felt an uplifting feeling. He opened his eyes, and saw Ra'id focusing hard, using his elements, pushing air towards Leinad.

Leinad slowly landed lightly on the ground,

"I owe you one, Ra'id. Thanks for saving my life." He bowed down on one knee and clenched his three fingered hand, and crossed it across his chest. He bowed his head towards Ra'id.

So this is how it feels to be King. Thought Ra'id, and he forced Leinad up.

"Don't worry, I just hope you'll save my life when I'm in danger," Ra'id spoke in a friendly voice. But, Ra'id could see behind Leinad's shoulder the body of the Batorat rising from the ground. It stood to its full height of four meters and prepared to breath fire. Ra'id reacted quickly. He engulfed the head of the Batorat with stone, preventing it from breathing. The Batorat keeled over within seconds, dead.

Leinad looked over his shoulder to see the body the Batorat collapse on the ground,

"I'm lucky you're on my side." He chuckled. The battle field looked grim. Boulders scattered the room, along with wounded people. Yavin forced enough energy to speak to Leinad,

"When can we eat? I'm starved..."

"Come. Let me show you the dining room." Every one of the companions hurried over, including Lemmor (who'd quickly recuperated from the hit), into a door beside heaps of metal. When they opened the door, a convection of tunnels revealed themselves,

"More tunnels?! I'm sick of trudging in the dark just to get from one room to another!" Complained Sasha. At least ten tunnels were in front of them, all in different directions.

"Na'yr, could you lead the way?" asked Ne'hoj. Na'yr walked in front of the gang. Suddenly, he started in one direction, following his nose.

"How do we know he's going the right way?" asked Tala silently to Se'maj. His voice boomed, even though he tried to whisper,

"He has super-sensitive senses. He is a tracker for the assassin, Fisk" Tala was frightened by the large voice.

Na'yr suddenly came to a stop. Three tunnels lay ahead of him. He lifted one finger, then the other two of his hand. Nobody would've seen anything but rock walls. However, Na'yr was different; he saw in highly detailed infrared vision. He quickly noticed the bright coloured figures moving on the other side of the room,

"We shall take the middle. It is the entrance to the kitchen," concluded Na'yr shortly. They hurried to center tunnel. Voices could be heard from the other side. Pots and pans being clanged all over rang through the room as the ten companions hurried through.

Na'yr squinted his sensitive eyes to the bright light. The walls were covered with white tiles that reflected the light in all directions. Most of the cooks had shades bent inward to protect their eyes. When the head chef (the one with a big hat) noticed the group, he wasn't surprised. The Xecwerians of the group visited the kitchen often, wondering what's for dinner.

Sasha was amazed. The whole kitchen had people working together to make meals. De-boning, frying, baking, garnishing. Everybody was doing something. They were so organized. Nobody bumped into the other, or walked quickly, even if there were such a large number of people. You'd be able to smell fish, sauces, veggies, and meats cooperating all at once, mustering a symphony of scents.

"We better hurry into the Dining Hall, before we get personally kicked out," said Gir'heg, smacking his lips. He obviously liked eating, though he was as thin as a twig. He continued to speak, "Aus'auj, could you whip up a special meal for," he spoke to the head chef. He clenched his three fingers, and pointed to the humans behind him,

"You know… the Chosen. I know I can count on you to make it special." He gave him a firm pat on the back. Aus'auj nodded several times He ushered his companions out of the room and into the Dining Hall.

Once the group had exited the kitchen, a being emerged from the shadows. It hurried over to Aus'auj, whispered some words, and handed him a black bottle. It hurried out of the room.

Yavin couldn't believe his eyes. The hall was so vast, about one hundred meters deep, with five long tables placed vertically. People sat on benches on each side of each table. They had dashing clothes. Some wore sparkling clothes, and the women wore skirts that dazzled in the light. The men wore dark green and black pants. Everyone was eager to eat, but they still took the chance to socialize. Some spoke English, others spoke different languages, such as Latin and Xecwerianish. A long table lay horizontal in front of the companions.

"Your clothes are in your rooms; Ne'hoj will show you the way. A wash basin will be there too, so you can freshen up in your quarters. Be back here in an hour." Ordered Lemmor, as every one of the friends dispersed into different directions. The remaining four followed Ne'hoj. He walked through a narrow doorway, and walked down the hall. There, four rooms lay with steel doors. The insides each had several bolts and locks. Ne'hoj designated each of them to their rooms, and left. In each room were stone walls, a soft bed, a washroom at the side, a bureau and a water basin. On the bed were neatly folded clothes, and beside them were a belt and silver dagger. The companions shut their doors and got to work quickly.

Half an hour later, they had themselves washed after they had checked their rooms. It took them another fifteen minutes to get the clothes on. It took a confusing pattern finally to get dressed. They each hurried out into the Dining Hall, following the same path as Ne'hoj had shown them. The dagger was neatly strapped under their clothes, in case of danger. Tala thought it was hazardous, so she didn't carry one.

They finally reached the Dining Hall, and all of them looked different. Sasha wore long, purple dress, with short sleeves. Her hair was hanging off the side, curled. The upper part of the dress had swirls on it. Ra'id wore a red shirt with a tuxedo over it. He had black pants down to his shoes, which were polished to shine. Yavin wore a white shirt, black pants, and black shoes. He didn't like this ensemble because it made him look plain. Tala wore a smaller dress of Sasha, but it was sky blue.

When the four companions met up, the other six were there. They wore tuxedoes, some white, grey and black. They all had their hair combed, so they didn't look unprofessional. Sasha finally noticed what Raghouik was trying to say. He had said the people of the planet were elegant, and now, with their peculiar eyes, and three fingers they looked elegant. In fact, they looked like they were a successful branch of human eugenics!

The group took their seats at the table in front of them. It was privately reserved for them. Leinad stood up, tapped his glass three times, and waited for silence. Then, he spoke up,

"Good evening, Blavarians. I just wanted to make a toast to the Chosen, for their first meal in Xecwer, and also to have defeated a monstrous creature; the Batorat." Everyone gasped and started to whisper to one another.

"Silence!" Boomed Se'maj.

"Thank you, Se'maj. Now, if it weren't for these four, I wouldn't be here right now. So let's give them a round of applause," finished Leinad, and he started clapping his hands. Everybody followed his suit, and clapped. The four companions were speechless.

"Now let the Dinner begin!" Cried Leinad. Waiters flowed out of doors behind them, holding trays, and pots. Five waiters came to their table, and laid the food in front of them.

"Let's start with the appetizers!" said Gir'heg, and a waiter opened a large tray. On it, were slices of pumpernickel bread, buttered in milk butter, and on top of it were snail shells. In the shells were pieces of orange along with the snail.

"Escargot au Laitier. Bon appétit!" Replied the waiter in a thick accent. Sasha didn't like the look of it,

"Do we have to eat it?!" demanded Sasha.

"You'll love it!" replied Ne'hoj. A Xecwerian came by with a spoon. He tried one snail.

"Whoa! Whoa! This is our food, bub! Get your own!" Exclaimed Yavin, waving his arms to shoo him away. His hands crackled with lightening. Obviously scared, the man ran away.

"Yavin, that guy was testing for poison. Next time someone dressed neatly comes by, let him check the food." Said Na'yr in a repulsive tone.

Everyone started eating the snails. They had a tangy taste, yet tasted of seafood. Then, the shell added a bit of crunchiness. Once the shells were gone, they wolfed down the bread. When everybody was finished their appetizers, Gir'heg opened another tray. It had a salmon, completely de-boned, sliced into cubes, and stuffed with salted mashed potatoes, garnished with gravy. Lemmor took a knife and divided the salmon evenly, leaving some pieces for someone to test.

Another man came by, and he tested the salmon. He savoured it, and chewed it thoughtfully. Ra'id quickly pulled out his knife and fork. He tried to pierce the salmon, but a strong force took over. The gauntlet was fighting back, trying to control Ra'id, for his sake. Suddenly, the tester's eyes widened, and he fell back.

*   *   *   *

"What is the meaning of this!?" Se'maj hollered to Aus'auj from the other side of the door. The four companions were listening in on the conversation after dinner. Some one tried to poison them during the dinner that passed. Once the food-tester dropped dead, gasps echoed throughout the vast hall. Thanks to Ra'id's gauntlet, he was still alive. The companions were forced to shuffle themselves out of the room to have a strict talk with the cook. The conversation had been going on for hours.

"I swear I have nothing to do with this!" said Aus'auj in his thick accent from a nation that wasn't from earth.

"Well, how do you suppose the poison slipped into the food?!" demanded Leinad from inside. Questions were being thrown at Aus'auj at a repetitive rate. The two friends were trying to trick him into spilling the beans. They asked questions back and forth, and Lemmor jotted quick notes in the back of the room.

"The poison might not have been a poison; maybe too much of one ingredient slipped in?" Stuttered Aus'auj, trying to worm his way out of this mess.

"What kind of ingredient could be able to poison someone with an overdose?! The recipe Gir'heg had asked you to do included no such ingredients!" Shouted Leinad. Aus'auj started to back away behind the kitchen table, fear struck in his eyes. Lemmor seized his chance. He rubbed his fingers against his forehead, and a purple glow illuminated the room. Suddenly, Aus'auj was lifted from the ground surrounded by a purple sphere. He contorted in all directions.

From outside, Ra'id could hear an agonizing cry of desperation fill the air. A gasp for breath, then nothing. Back in the kitchen, Aus'auj lay on the ground, muttering under his breath. He was in a deep trance.

"It was Sa'rin. She was the one who did it. She told me what to do, and handed me this bottle," Aus'auj continued, and pulled out a bottle half full of a black substance. Leinad slowly read the bottles contents,

"Sa'rin couldn't have done it. She's my Chief advi-"

"Shhh! He still has something to say!" whispered Lemmor. Aus'auj continued,

"She spoke about the return of strength, and ran out of the room to the~" He stopped and fell unconscious.

"Where? Where did she go, you daft fool!?" exclaimed Lemmor, trying to shake him awake.

"Enough, Lemmor! We have bigger problems. We need to find Sa'rin. She could kill us all." Said Leinad, completely disappointed in her and himself. He whispered some words Ra'id couldn't depict from behind the door. Suddenly, they heard walking towards the door.

"Sasha, make us invisible!" Ra'id ordered. Everyone disappeared in time, and the two other ones walked through the door. They hurried to their rooms.

The four companions that had eavesdropped hurried back to their quarters. Their eyes drooped from being so tired. They all shut the door after the other. Sasha changed into some sleeping robes on the bed, and went straight to sleep. Yavin explored his room a bit more, and drifted to sleep. Tala just dropped onto the bed. But Ra'id changed into his robes, went to the bed, but thought.

What would Sa'rin have to do with anything? Ra'id knew deep within his memories he would find the reason, because something was evil about Sa'rin, something that seemed obvious, yet mysterious. Ra'id decided to sleep on it.

Ra'id stood in a dimly lit room. The same room he dreamed about the day before the sleepover. His features were invisible, and he felt as if he was there. Suddenly, a low creek pierced the silence, and light filled the room. But the doorway was covered by a large, towering figure. A being from the opposite side of the room stood up from his throne.

"So, how was the search? Is the Power Orb with you? Or do I have to split your skull open with this Sklitificu Staff?!" The figure from the opposite room spoke with a raspier voice,

"We tried to dispatch the group after eliminating Earth, but they easy destroyed the finest breed of Megascororpio. Maybe we could try the Arachanecis~"

"Enough of your useless babbling!! You went and let the Megascororpio fight against four experienced chosen ones! Do you have the Power Orb at least?!" The figure started mumbling, and then spoke up,

"Uh...Uh... No, but we managed to capture Raghouik." Murmured the figure,

"But you didn't get the Orb back. And you know what the consequences are..."

He lifted a long staff from beside his throne. The end of it glowed with a bright luminous light.

"No! Not yet! I've inquired information from Sa'rin... She's found the Orb," the light suddenly dimmed, and the staff slowly dropped down.

"The Orb can be acquired tonight. Sa'rin will contact you. All you need is to give her a militia. She'll bring the Orb within the next month."

"You better be right, or your head will be served to me on a platter."

Ra'id woke up to a sudden humming sound. He looked around. Under his sheet, a turquoise colour glowed with swerving patterns. He lifted his hand to see the source; the Gauntlet of Blavarix. The swerves were replaced with words. Ra'id read them out loud:

"'Whenever you are sleeping, keep one eye peering, for as they've reckoned, she'll freeze you in seconds.'" The vision suddenly disappeared, and the curves reappeared on to the gauntlet.

That's it! The last time the gauntlet gave me a message, it told me to befriend and beware.

But Ra'id didn't know was Sa'rin was marching down with a small army consisting of twenty large Xecwerians, plated in thick armour and armed with weapons. Sa'rin was leading them straight to the Blavarial community, ready to take back the Power Orb.

*   *   *   *

Ra'id rushed out of the room with a loaf of bread in his mouth. He had overslept, and now he was late for training.

"My second day, and already, I'm late!" muttered Ra'id under his breath as he tore another piece of bread. The hallways continued in an unending maze. Thirty minutes later, Ra'id reached the Orb chamber. The two Orbs floated lonely at the center of the room. They flickered to his entrance as a greeting. He hurried to the other side. Once he reached the other end, he placed his hand over a hand-print, and the doors parted.

"Ra'id, you're late! You must've slept in haven't you?" Said Leinad cheerily. He welcomed Ra'id into the training fields.

Ra'id and Leinad fought with their blades until noon. Ra'id won most fights, but he was left drained of his energy after. The gauntlet was still trying to possess Ra'id, but his inner willpower kept it from doing so. Later, Leinad explained some history,

"Xecweranites have visited Earth for the past several millennia. We usually check Earth in case other extra terrestrials invade it for some strange reasons,"

"You mean you guys have been protecting our planet?"

"Yep, that's how it's been for the past several thousand years. But, once Crenar came to power as the tyrant king of Xecwer, he rarely cared for earthlings." Ra'id was still amazed by the fact that aliens actually did come to Earth. Leinad continued,

"We blew our cover several times, however…"

"When was that?"

"The first time wasn't such a big problem, because the humans who had discovered us thought we were gods."

"Who?"

"Well, I'm not sure who they were, but they did seem interested in our eyes..." Leinad pointed to his eyes. Ra'id immediately remembered where he saw it before,

"That's the eye of Horus! The Egyptians worshipped him. He was the Egyptian god of flight!"

"That's it! Since then, they've been mimicking our eyes. However, we didn't arouse much suspicion of life outside of Earth. But, the second time we were caught, it was about five thousand years later,"

"What happened?"

"One of our crafts crashed more recently in a place called... Roswell, I think."

"So you were the ones who started all this talk about extraterrestrials..."

Ra'id suddenly realised that, even if he had been living with extra terrestrials for the past few days, that aliens were in fact real and not hoaxes.

"What I really wanted to teach you today is about -" he looked carefully around, as if someone was eavesdropping,

"Magic!" He slowly whispered. He rushed towards the Orb chamber. He ran out, holding the Power Orb. It writhed with life within Leinad's palm.

"When you use your power, you use lots of energy, right?"

"Of course!" Leinad took the Orb, and placed it over one hand.

"Now, have you tried to light a room with fire?"

"Yes, but the room was still engulfed in darkness,"

"*Reparafuego Brilliance!*" Pronounced Leinad.

The orb jumped in his hand, awakened by his words. It began spin violently, and Leinad was forced to let go. It hovered above his hand. Ra'id noticed something *different* about this procedure. It didn't begin sucking the energy out of things. Instead, it used its own.

A sudden flame appeared on Leinad's palm, flickered there for a second, then brightened with a luminous glow. The light brightened the training grounds. Ra'id closed his eyes, but the light continued to penetrate his eyelids. He closely covered his eyes with his hands, until a dim light replaced the blinding sparkle.

"That was amazing!" Exclaimed Ra'id.

"The other thing is I didn't use an excruciating amount of energy." Pointed Leinad, then he handed Ra'id a list with strange characters of a language. They resembled Egytian hieroglyphics, but not quite the same,

"What do these scribbles mean?" Ra'id asked as he peered down on to the sheet. He couldn't understand anything written on it.

"Oh, sorry 'bout that. *Revelendo Undaga!*" Suddenly, words that were legible to Ra'id replaced the symbols.

"These are spells you can use with the Power Orb. Learn them by tomorrow." Leinad dismissed Ra'id. What puzzled Ra'id was the fact Leinad was teaching him many things, yet he just started.

Sasha joined up with him, and explained what happened that day. They had asked her to use her power to add force into her weapon. Then, she had to fight Fisk with a stick, and to try to penetrate to his body. But, Fisk used his barriers stop the blows. Only twice did Sasha get through. They both hurried to their rooms and sponged themselves down. They cleaned up and proceeded quickly through the day. They enjoyed dinner, with some mashed potatoes smothered in gravy along with a nice cocktail, a combination of cranberry, strawberry and raspberry. The companions got escorted to their rooms safely, and fell asleep soundly.

Ra'id slept uneasily, however.

Why am I being taught so many things at once? Is it Leinad's teaching habit, or is it for a good reason? Is he preparing me for something that they've seen? Something that could end the lives of hundreds of Blavarians?

*   *   *   *

"Who's there?" Lay'tor, the night guardian of the Orb chamber, demanded. His eyes had developed the ability to see in the dark. The reason why was because he's part Hobgoblin. He was guarding the quiet scene, as usual, but the shadows seemed to have shifted. An eerie darkness continued to surround him, unlike any before.

"Who's there?" Repeated Lay'tor. No response. He backed himself to the corner of the room as a shadow of a monster struck the wall. Ravaged teeth were shown with slimy mucus dripping down from the fangs. The curved scythe claws of the beast frightened Lay'tor even more.

Out of nowhere, a slippery voice was heard,

"Now, comradesssss… Now!" The raspy voice echoed through Lay'tor's mind, only to be interrupted by a shadow jumping out of the dark. Almost immediately, Lay'tor retaliated with a brisk plunge of the sword. A deafening crackle echoed through the room, caused by the splitting of its skull. Lay'tor started breathing heavily. Once again, a form leaped out of the darkness. Lay'tor's thrust was halted by a hard Xecweranite shield. Lay'tor simply knocked the shield aside and struck again. It divided with a deep sucking sound. Then, a large line of Xecwerians formed horizontally, and, without provocation, they charged, spears at the ready. Lay'tor was astonished. He had no way to defend himself from eight men, let alone defend the Orbs too.

He started at the side, slashing his way through. Most retaliated. A strong torrent of thuds smashed Lay'tor's Xecweranite shield, leaving occasional dents. Lay'tor then lifted his head from his shield and swiped at the nearest thing. It released a cry of disgusted pain. He stabbed here and there. Ten minutes later, with sweat rolling down his forehead, he knocked out the last intruder with a blow from his shield. The body of the interloper fell limp, and collapsed to the ground.

Lay'tor celebrated his win with shouts of triumph. But his victory was short lived. Out of the shifting shadows emerged a dark figure. It spoke with a slippery voice,

"You may have disposed my army, but you have nothing to be happy about…" Mystifyingly, the being disappeared then reappeared among the shadows.

*   *   *   *

Ra'id felt a strange change in the air that night. A chill crept down his neck. His heightened sense of smell tasted the air. A pungent scent burned his nostrils. It was a very strong smell. The smell of fresh blood.

Chapter 10

"Now, Ra'id, did you memorize the list of spells I gave you yesterday?" asked Leinad, beads of sweat rolling down his forehead. He had duelled Ra'id earlier that day to train his swordsman skills. Leinad was the one that learned the most, however,

"Of course I memorized them! I'm excited about learning Magic!" Ra'id replied a tad louder than necessary.

"Well, just to test you, I'll ask you some questions. We don't want kids walking around blasting everything in sight. Which spell moves liquids?" Asked Leinad.

"*Aquego Arosess*, of course," he asked another question,

"Which spell represents control?"

"*Commando*." Replied Ra'id. Leinad was convinced.

"I'll let you practice with the Orb until tomorrow, on one condition; you won't show the Power Orb to anyone, and use it only on unanimated objects," he paused for a while, as if he hesitated to say something, then responded, "Class dismissed."

Ra'id pondered why he dismissed him early, and headed out, only to see his companions heading out too.

"What're you guys doing out early?" Asked Ra'id as he caught up to them.

"Well, Gir'heg handed me a pouch of coins to go buy some targets and Blavarite tipped arrows. He wants Tala to experiment with her stones he gave her to hit targets," Replied Yavin, explaining what happened that day. They first charged their weapons. Then, with practice equipment, they hit targets. They headed back to their quarters, but Ra'id stopped by the Orb chamber to pick up the Power Orb. He placed his hand over the door, and let the door's two rusty pieces awake in his presence.

He peered into the large hallway,

"Hello, anyone here?" He asked as he entered the gigantic chamber. He looked at the center of the room, where the Orbs should've been. But there was nothing. Nothing at all but the ominous floating noise of the Trait Orb. Its purple light glowed lonely without the Power Orb's blue aura.

"Where could it be? I saw it just yesterday..." He said to himself in the hall.

He rushed to Leinad's office to notify the disappearance of the Orb. He hurried through the halls past the bustling Blavarians. When he reached the office, he heard voices from the other side. The door was shut tight with a sign notifying to keep out. Ra'id thickened the air to hear what was being said:

Leinad's muffled voice was heard discordantly: "Explain yourself, Sa'rin!"

A greasy voice filled the air: "I'm sorry, Leinad, but Crenar controlled me with his powers, and forced me to do his biddings."

"Are you sure? How can I tell you're telling the truth?"

There was a long pause. Someone started mumbling, but the words were incomprehensible.

Leinad, who didn't seem to notice the indistinct words, spoke up: "I guess I'll have to have you arrested and send you to the dungeon..."

But the words were stopped by a sudden buzzing. Ra'id couldn't identify it. But it was clearly obvious to Leinad. Sa'rin was using the Power Orb. From beneath her cloak, Sa'rin lifted the Power Orb, then said,

"You cannot stop me now! I'll destroy you and your little rebellion!" Then, over the buzzing and whirling wind, Ra'id heard Sa'rin holler,

"Nsve Arosess!" Ra'id was puzzled. He knew the words were Xecweranish, but the words didn't seem to be on the lists of spells Leinad had given him. Whether Ra'id knew the spell or not, he had to help Leinad fast. With his wind power, he compressed air to blast the door down. He charged in, only to see it was too late. Sa'rin had already escaped, and Leinad was being attacked by many maroon coloured beings, wrinkled like raisins. The slippery voice of the gauntlet whispered in his mind, Zombies…

"Go catch Sa'rin!" cried Leinad over the howls of the zombies. He slashed two into pieces, but the body parts crept along the floor. Ra'id didn't need to answer. He blasted two of them with fire, and opened the earth for them to re-enter. The demons quickly scrambled to the hole and vanished without a trace.

Without much hesitation, Ra'id jumped out the window. He saw Sa'rin hundreds of metres ahead of him, dashing like a hare in the valley of the Blavarians. Ra'id threw a cushion of air in front of him and started hovering. He parted the earth here and there where Sa'rin stepped. Sa'rin looked back at her pursuer and with a surprised expression, lifted the Orb and pronounced a spell,

"Fuego Reparaquego!" A sudden red glow surrounded the Power Orb, and with some time, it focused its energy. Then it released energy and a stream of lava shot out. Grass and trees withered at the presence of this stream, and it was directed right at Ra'id.

He remained calm, however. The gauntlet took over Ra'id's consciousness like a parasitic virus. Ra'id knocked on his fire powers. He inhaled. A sharp sucking sound filled the air. The lava was absorbed into Ra'id, giving him new energy. Then, with a brisk movement, he shot the stream out from his hands and back at Sa'rin.

With her back turned she couldn't see the oncoming lava. It struck her right in the spine. Sa'rin fell back in agonizing pain.

Ra'id rejoiced in his capture. But his smile faded away. Sa'rin muttered a few words, and the burns vanished, and Sa'rin was back on her feet running again. Am I imagining things? Thought Ra'id, seeing Sa'rin running at his normal pace. Leinad's list didn't include many spells that Sa'rin has been casting. Is Leinad trying to hide spells from me, or is he protecting me from something evil?

Still pondering his thoughts, Ra'id pursued his enemy even further. He entered a thick forest, which was hard to keep track of Sa'rin from there. Instead, Ra'id shot a strong jet of water to slow down Sa'rin. The rain pounded Sa'rin like a torrent of water, yet she still kept the pace. She hurried over to a thick canopy, where she knew Ra'id would never find her. But she didn't know Ra'id. Ra'id shot fire here and there onto canopies too thick for his water. Down below the canopy, Sa'rin could hear the crackling of fire. She looked above, and to her surprise a fireball was shot strait at her. She stood up and froze the fire itself.

Ra'id was astounded. How could Sa'rin use powers without the Power Orb's spells? Or was Sa'rin gifted with the power of the Orb before? Ra'id thought. Thousands of questions continued to pop up in Ra'id's mind, but he just kept following the enemy. The forest never seemed to end, and it ended up with Ra'id setting the whole wood ablaze. He finally found his enemy, only to be scurrying into the desert.

*   *   *   *

"Where is Ra'id?!" demanded Yavin. Yavin had been worrying and waiting for Ra'id to come out of his quarters the next morning. He wanted to walk with Ra'id to training, because he usually got lost. Also, Ra'id was his best friend, no matter how much they'd bother each other. They always would stick together. Yet, that day, Ra'id wasn't stumbling out of bed. Not even some murmuring was heard. Just a dead silence. Yavin couldn't take it any longer. He twisted the doorknob with a vigorous turn and had thrust the door open.

Nobody was in the room. Ra'id's bed was untouched; the papers were all left in a nice pile. Everything was too quiet, as if it was unlived.

"Ra'id, are you here?" Yavin asked as he inched his eyes across the door. Yavin found Ra'id's scimitar's pommel underneath the bed,

"Why wouldn't he have his scimitar with him…" muttered Yavin, totally confused. Yavin rushed out of the room to the Training Grounds. He sped through the hallways, rounded the bend a couple of times and nearly hit some walking pedestrians.

At the Training Grounds, Yavin scanned the arena. No sign of Ra'id. Yavin rushed over to Leinad with a questioning expression on his face.

"What's wrong?" Asked Leinad, reading Yavin's mind,

"I can't find Ra'id!" He exclaimed.

"I couldn't find him this morning either. I think he might be training outside," said Leinad with a very unsure tone.

"Honestly, where was the last place you saw him?" demanded Yavin. Leinad couldn't hold in the truth much longer,

"Ok, ok, I'll tell you. The last time I saw him was when he leaped out the window to catch Sa'rin…"

"Sa'rin? Why?" Questioned Yavin. Leinad replied in a guilty manner,

"Sa'rin stole the Power Orb," Yavin let out a gasp, and then Leinad continued, "and she suddenly escaped nowhere to be found. Ra'id followed. Now he's somewhere in Xecwer."

There was a long pause after that. It was interrupted by Gir'heg's consistent calls. Yavin took a look at Leinad and walked towards Gir'heg's lesson. Targets were set up in a row, and Yavin strung his bow with a Blavarial arrow.

*   *   *   *

Water trickled down Ra'id's wrist as he sipped some of it from his cupped hands. He had been travelling in the desert for a week already. Sa'rin was already kilometres ahead of him, using the Orb to ease her journey. Ra'id slowly hovered and used his fire powers to reduce the heat. But, he had to make his own water. He had encountered scorpions, dingoes, and several other creatures he couldn't describe. He usually would flee from them, but if they attacked, he'd bury them in earth, then hide behind the nearest cactus.

It was rough in the desert. In the middle of the day, Ra'id would have to make shelter out of a thin layer of water, which kept him cool. But he couldn't just wait, or Sa'rin would get too far, so he moved day and night. Now, Ra'id was hovering at a high speed to catch Sa'rin. It would only take hours for him to catch up.

The next night, Ra'id had zoomed across most of the desert and was now entering the Dry Plains of Xecwer. Ra'id knew this place from maps he studied in his quarters. He also knew it would give him time to catch Sa'rin, because the flat plains gave him a wide range to hover over, while the grass slowed Sa'rin. Ra'id now caught up with Sa'rin's footprints, but they seemed old.

As Ra'id was cooling himself down, a small owl hooted to him. It jumped out of its nest and hopped towards him.

"Shhhh! Scram! You don't want coyotes to come, do you?" Whispered Ra'id in a friendly manner. A demeanour of friendliness seemed to spur in Ra'id's chest, but the gauntlet thought otherwise,

This isn't the brightest idea… For your own sake, please do not befriend this fiend. Ra'id put this matter to an end. However, his gauntlet stirred strangely, not liking it. He welcomed the owl to his lap and he fell into a deep sleep.

"Are you sure that we must?" The voice was strangely familiar.

"Yes. This is absolutely necessary. It's been a week already. Who says Sa'rin didn't send out a message to Crenar. I know Sa'rin is very powerful," Leinad had joined the conversation. Ra'id could see their silhouettes in the dark room. Se'maj spoke up,

"What does Sa'rin have that Ra'id can't handle?"

"First of all, Sa'rin is a Catalyst,"

"What?! When were you going to tell me?"

"She never told me so, but I knew she was human for a reason,"

"She has five fingers?" Se'maj was totally surprised.

"Of course! I automatically speculated that she was on Xecwer for a reason. There are only a handful of humans on Xecwer, and all of them are Catalysts."

"I knew that much. Why didn't you tell me this information?"

"I don't know! It slipped my mind, I guess..."Leinad felt slightly guilty.

"How was it that you found out she was a Catalyst?"

"When I had confronted her in my office, she cast one of the Dark spells,"

"So? That doesn't prove any~"

"It does! Only Catalysts can cast them! I'm sure of it, Se'maj! I didn't teach Ra'id those spells, luckily~" Se'maj had to interrupt,

"You taught him some MAGIC?!" He fumed.

"Se'maj, it was needed! I sensed that a great danger was going disrupt our lives! Ra'id needed the extra training, and it needed to be done as soon as possible," Se'maj didn't comment this at all. He waited quietly for Leinad's following statement,

"I didn't teach him the power of the Dark spells. I knew it was too dangerous for him. However, he has a way to access these spells..."Se'maj was clearly puzzled.

"The ~" He stopped talking.

"What is it~" Leinad stopped Se'maj. He looked around the room; he clearly sensed something. Ra'id gasped,

"There's something in the air tonight. This discussion must be held at another time..."

*   *   *   *

Now being two weeks since his vision, Ra'id could see Sa'rin's body trudging through the grass tirelessly. He had grown close friends with the little owl. It would always perch on his head and sit there while Ra'id hovered over the grass. It made occasional hoots. It usually flew during the night for mice and other rodents. It actually made Ra'id happier to have this playful companion.

The Dry Plains didn't feel as bad as it sounded. The grass was pretty long, and the fields were flat, but the weather wasn't so bad, and the humidity was average. Ra'id hovered pleasantly over the fields. Sa'rin's figure always seemed to come closer, so Ra'id started devising plans.

First, I'll open a pit below Sa'rin. That will give me a bit of time to fill it with water. If that attempt to drown fails, then I'll shoot fire at the water to create a fog. I'll use that as a distraction for me to steal the Orb... Ra'id revised the plan, making sure the consequences weren't too bad,

But, if I don't get the Orb, Sa'rin would be ready to kill me. I guess it's now or never.

Two days later of hovering, restoring energy, and devising plans, Ra'id finally caught up to Sa'rin. He was only metres behind her now, and he cautioned the owl not to hoot. He slowly hovered over to Sa'rin, and then sprung his plan. The earth beneath Sa'rin fell open, and then Ra'id flooded it with water. Ra'id could see Sa'rin treading the freezing water he had sent. Ra'id summoned his fire powers in one hand, and water in the other. He then clapped the two hands together to shoot a stream of hot mist towards Sa'rin. Cries of agony were heard as Sa'rin closed her eyes before they got singed. Ra'id seized his chance. He grabbed the Power Orb with his air powers from Sa'rin's hand. Victory was his! Once he had the Orb, he went to entangle Sa'rin, so he could bring her to Blavarians, where her sentence would be decided from there. Instead, his gauntlet quickly overtook his body entirely. It forced to words through Ra'id's mind:

"Paraquego Arosess!" Sa'rin rose from the water. Then, a beam of light struck her the chest. Seconds later, all liquids were released from her body, turning her to dust.

Ra'id was astonished. He could feel the power of death that had just left his palm. The gauntlet felt a sick satisfaction at the death of Sa'rin.

"What… is this Magic, this evil Power? Was Leinad protecting me from this? Are these the 'Dark spells' Leinad had discussed?"

Ra'id hovered back to the direction he came from. Now that he had the Power Orb, he could now return to the Blavarial Community. But, as he hovered from the grass, a crisp crackle was heard. He looked around, confused. The owl suddenly hooted loudly, raising its neck. Ra'id looked around, and saw nothing but the swaying grass. Suddenly, it flew from Ra'id's shoulder and sunk into the grass.

"Come back!" Ra'id called to his companion. But not even a hoot had replied. Ra'id waited there in dead silence, until he heard movement in the grass. He whipped his head back, only to find nothing. Then it hit him. He knew what surrounded him. Invisible spirits, those who work for King Crenar!

"Embèlié I Paritri!" Shouted Ra'id. Suddenly, figures started to reform all over. Some were black beasts with fiery eyes and twist horns. Just the look of them could give nightmares. There were the ugliest of Hobgoblins, with slime oozing from battle wounds. They all smiled a malevolent grin. Ra'id was horror-struck. One of them leaped at him. The fear in Ra'id's heart suddenly triggered his powers. A deep fog emitted from his hands, and the hobgoblin missed his target. Ra'id could sense them around, because the air grew chilly every extra moment he spent in their presence. He heard a low howl, and drew his dagger. Its blade reflected the face of an oncoming beast. Immediately, he spun around and plunged the dagger in its direction. It grazed its elbow, but a howl of excruciating pain echoed through the air. Another beast behind him wound his legs, and collided with Ra'id's head, and he fell unconscious.

*   *   *   *

"What? You want Fish, Na'yr, Tala, Yavin and I to go and search for the Powder Orb?!" Exclaimed Sasha at the top of her lungs to Leinad. It seemed like she was going to blow her top.

"It's Fisk, not Fish," corrected Ne'hoj angrily. Gir'heg chimed in,

"It's the Power Orb," Sasha was in Leinad's office with the other Catalysts and the Chosen of the Traits Orb. The room was very crowded and crunched. The group was debating about going to retrieve Ra'id and the Orb or not.

"The child is much too audacious! Why waste our time?" pointed out Se'maj, who was irate of being interrupted during a meeting with Lemmor. They were having a heated discussion about several war strategies until Gir'heg burst through the door, explaining their predicament.

"I want all of you to settle down now. Se'maj may you?" Leinad leered his head towards Se'maj,

"Of course," then, he lifted his voice and boomed across the tight room, "Quiet all of you!" The windows started to rattle. A dead silence filled the room. "Thank you," said Se'maj silently. Leinad continued to speak,

"Now, I'll need all of your help now. Since we lost Lay'tor, there has been no one to take his place in guarding the Traits Orb. Any volunteers?" Na'yr's three-fingered hand shot straight up, but Leinad added, "Besides Na'yr, Fisk, Sasha, Yavin and Tala?" The room remained silent. Only three candidates were left.

"I've got the army to attend to," strummed up Se'maj as an excuse. Lemmor also spoke up,

"Se'maj can't handle the whole army by himself. That's why I'm here!" Gir'heg knew this was coming,

"I guess I'll have to be appointed night-guard." Leinad look surprised,

"All against the election of Gir'heg's position say 'Nay'" No one spoke up, "Then it is final. Gir'heg will join the other night guards. Good luck." Leinad ushered Gir'heg out of the room to go and tell the news to the Night Guard's Lounge.

"Now, back to this matter about Ra'id and the Power Orb's disappearances. You five will go and seek Ra'id wherever he may be, and retrieve the Power Orb. Simple enough?" Leinad asked the remaining people in the room. They nodded their heads sequentially, but Tala also had several questions on her mind,

"Why do we have to get the Power Orb?" Squeaked little Tala, but she continued, "It's not as if Cretin – I mean Crenar," all of the Xecwerians winced at his name, "can force the Orb to grant powers, can he?" Leinad took a long pause before answering,

"You're right, the King can't force the Power Orb into doing anything, but there's one thing he can do with it," before Leinad gave the answer away, he glanced at his fellow companions whether he should tell them or not. They each gave him a simple nod,

"That one thing is… the Power Orb not only gives away powers, but it can be used to cast spells that cause all sorts of things. I think Raghouik might have mentioned it to you…" The children realized what he was talking about:

The people who do not control the power in trusted from the Orb can use its power, only if it's at hand, the words echoed in the companions minds as they recalled the raspy voice of Raghouik.

"I have a question," said Yavin, "How come the Power orb can control everything, yet it can't do things at its own free will?"

"The only thing the Power Orb decide to do is ~" Leinad was interrupted by a quick rap against the metal door,

"Enter." Gir'heg walked in,

"The Night Guards accepted my recruit," he said.

"As I was saying, the Power Orb can only decide the people of which to bestow powers upon," Leinad finished this quickly, almost seeming as if leaving a very important part out. Gir'heg noticed this automatically and said,

"Aren't you forgetting something Leinad? The Orb can do many more things, such as the Creation?"

"The Creation?" Questioned Sasha.

"Yes the Creation. Gather 'round now," Gir'heg beckoned everyone to take a seat and c move closer,

"I may not be a great storyteller like Se'maj, but I know my history, and I'm going to tell you all about it whether Leinad likes it or not," Gir'heg took a long breath, and prepared himself for his spiel,

"Now to answer your question, Sasha, the Power Orb can control who it bestows its powers upon, but, unlike Leinad said, it can control anything unnatural that may occur, such as disappearances of people to monster hurricanes.

"You might want to know what the Creation was. The Creation was when the Universe started. In the time before time, there was nothing but a divine Being called Odyleus. This divine Being had power beyond your imagination, but it was never used. One time, however, this Being, decided he wanted to share his power with creatures, so he created the universe, with nothing in it however, just a black pit. He decided to share his powers with a ball. Not just any ball, but the Power Orb. He decided to fill it with his power so it could be with him too.

"See, what the Odyleus didn't know was that the Power Orb could think freely. It didn't just float and create stars out of thin air. It could think and devise plans. So, instead of staying with the Odyleus, the Power Orb exhausted its powers by creating everything we know about today, except for your planet. After using all of its energy, the Power Orb descended from the heavens and landed in the hands of Crenar, Odyleus' son. Back in that time, Crenar was no evil scum, but a ruler of a peaceful land. Once the Orb fit into his hands (it had shrunk because of the loss of energy), he was lost in a trance. He was given the choice to choose a power, to become a Catalyst of energy and matter. He thought of the power that would protect his planet from any evil."

"What was it?" Demanded Tala. Gir'heg continued,

"It was the power to control space itself. And the theory was that with the control of Space, Time followed in synchronization. So, he mastered his powers for hundreds of years~"

"How did he live so long?" Asked Sasha, continuously inquisitive. Gir'heg answered without hesitation,

"The Power Orb granted him nearly everlasting life. After hundreds of years, he grew greedy and selfish, and, in pursuit of eternal power, he created Magic," the word made Se'maj shudder, and Leinad gave a yelp.

"Magic?"

"He created Magic from the Xecweranish language. He overpowered the Orb with his Powers of Space and forced it to make a silent contract. The deal was the Power Orb would obey the holder as long as it spoke ancient Xecweranish. Then, the Power Orb will change the words into the thing itself. If I said 'Vento'" all of a sudden, a quick gust filled the air, and the room filled up with a swooping sound, "the Orb would produce a gust of wind. Depending on the willpower of the holder, the strength of the spell would be determined."

Yavin started to speak after the long pause,

"Gir'heg, I followed your whole story, but I didn't hear a thing about Earth and its creation."

"Several hundred years later, King Crenar created Earth using his spatial powers. He planned to use it and its inhabitants as his subjects. If anything were to be tested, Crenar would send it down to Earth. He influences people's dream, causing them to invent different things."

"When did Blavarix start rebelling?" Asked Sasha, who usually detested politics, was however, interested.

"Well, when King Crenar was well in his reign, he started recruiting Xecwerians as slaves. When Blavarix found this out, he banded with some of his companions, raided the fortress after many years of plans, and they fled to an underground path. You might be wondering who these companions were. Well, one was Raghouik," Tala piped up,

"You mean the shadow guy who brought us here from Earth?"

"Yep. When they touched the Power Orb, it sought out their pure hearts. It recalled the mistake it made, giving Crenar powers, so it surrendered its powers to Blavarix. They both had a power to choose. Raghouik selected Shadows, knowing the power over them controlled most things, and Blavarix couldn't decide. They fled from the fortress and started a small rebellion called 'The Blavarians'. King Crenar probably knows it exists. Later on, Blavarix took up arsenal making, and therefore teaching the whole colony how to defend themselves. Then, one night, the Power Orb woke in his slumber. It shook Xecwer with such thunderous force the Orb chamber was created. Blavarix remembered his chance to receive an impeccable power. Knowing his duty was one of the most important of all, he decided the power of Metal.

"Decades after the establishment of 'The Blavarians', Blavarix planned an attack. Crenar was too busy searching for the Orb; military affairs were no concern whatsoever. But before they could fight, they needed great weapons, beyond Crenar's control. Blavarix created the Gauntlet of which Ra'id owns. Since the energy of Blavarix was limited, he called for the Power Orb's energy. The amount of energy was so much, the leftovers floated in a purple mass of energy. It floated in the Orb chamber, awaiting its destiny. Raghouik used the Orb's powers to create the Sklitificu Staff." Tala was confused,

"What?"

"It was used to remove all of the flesh of the target, usually leaving it as a shell or skeleton," Yavin recalled their visit to the Ruins of Xecwer,

"So that's why everyone is left as skeletons in that large room, where Leinad found us."

"Yes, but I'll tell that tale after this one. The whole rebellion attacked during the night using shadows to conceal themselves. When they raided the fortress, King Crenar himself was there at the doorway. He immediately transferred the whole battle to a wide chamber in the community. He had also transferred some of his sleeping warriors over to the chamber. The war began. Raghouik and Blavarix held the battle to their favour. Crenar saw that the Staff was a powerful artefact. He got a hold of it within several days, and the battle was completely altered from then on. Within a week, the army was vanquished.

"And ever since then, Crenar has been in power with Sklitificu alongside his throne of dark power. Now that he has the Orb, he's going to create an army that'll destroy us all!"

"So who's with me?!" Demanded Fisk.

"I!" Each one of them hollered at the same time. With triumphant fists, they hurried over to the arsenal arena and started their work.

Chapter 11

Ra'id gazed ghostishly at his shamble body pass by, being carried by grotesque monsters. A very piquant smell infected the air while these ill at ease fiends muscled their way through the lofty grass. He couldn't establish whether he was dead or alive. The brutes carrying his flaccid cadaver resembled immense giants with oversized triangular heads. Even though midnight had fallen, their obscurity pierced the night, making him finally realise what pure darkness was...

Ra'id floated after the ghouls. As he swayed side to side, he noticed translucent arms flailing by his side. Astonished, he stopped in his tracks and observed his body. The whole corpse glowed bright blue in the dark, which seemed to be his only source of light. Its transparent appearance forced Ra'id to shudder, though the night air was clammy. I guess I'm already dead, thought Ra'id weakly as he continued to follow the beasts manipulating his lithesome corpse. Ra'id hurried to keep up with the evil beings, making sure not to touch them, though he probably would've passed right through them. As he grew nearer to the demons, he could hear them rasping for breath. The noise made him nauseated, as it sounded like a giant pig grunting and snuffling desperately for food. The only way the creatures communicated was with very rudimentary sign language and deep grunts.

Ra'id couldn't keep track of the time as he continued to follow his captors, though the sun was supposed to be peeking over the horizon by then. He continuously threw desperate glances towards the east end of the planet, wishing the rays of sun would lift his spirit (metaphorically speaking, that is). The hushed clad finally came to halt, and Ra'id noticed this when he passed right through the group. They knocked several times on to a large oaken door. Then, almost immediately, a flurry of cool air was forced out of the door and out into the warm night. The door swung vigorously to its side, almost knocked off its hinges. The group trudged into the fortress, and Ra'id narrowly slipped through it. A dark figure with neon green eyes approached them; it seemed as if a pair of eyes, however, floated towards them. It lifted a glowing red canister and let it float an entourage around the soundless group.

Several minutes later, the cylinder illuminated the room with a sky blue, and then it flickered between crimson and azure. Alarmed, the figure approached the destination of where the apparatus stopped and grasped into the pouch. It seemed excited to have found this thing, as if it had been searching for it for centuries. He stopped abruptly, and then stood there, bemused. His lifelong accomplishment was finally complete. Without looking as though it would jinx the instant, he let his hand mount from the sachet. Once it emerged, the walls glowed with its light. Ra'id had to swathe his eyes with his forearms, who was surprised to see radiance. As it faded away, he caught a glimpse of the source. A blue globe was elevated in the guard's palm, and he yelled triumphantly,

"Yes!!! WE HAVE IT! Undying power is... OURS!" A sudden roar of life filled the room, as many stumbling creatures roused themselves. The eyes all seemed to fall on the Orb, and the glinted pupils seemed to approach. The bestial monsters gave a few incomprehensible grunts, yet the Xecwerian responded gleefully,

"Dispose of the Catalyst; he is too much of a threat..." Then, he looked around as he was being watched suspiciously. Ra'id finally noticed, but reacted too late,

114

"Revilìé!" Immediately, Ra'id's body regained its solid form (the one that was ghostly) and the being laughed,

"And it looks like his soul has already been split. Let's think of ways to abolish him from the face of the universe." He pulled back his hand, and murmured some words. A high-pitched hum scratched the deadly silence. The Orb gained an orange coloured, and prepared to release the energy inside...

"No!" Hollered Ra'id, leaping to his feet. He suddenly realised he was in a tight white suit with rubber gloves on. Thick drops of sweat rolled down his face, and he lay there, stunned. Suddenly, a recollection of what had happened the previous night came to him as hard thuds echoed from the back of his head. Wave after wave of pain issued from a hefty bump in his skull. Regaining his senses, he looked around the room. It was illuminated with white unlike the hall he had dreamt of. Absolutely nothing in the hostile quarters wasn't gleaming with white, blinding Ra'id. It was completely shut off, with no exits whatsoever that were noticeable. He searched as if he were a mouse trying to escape a large residence. But suddenly a booming voice repeated itself throughout the vast expanse.

Ra'id wasn't totally reassured whether the scientists of the fortress had conducted any experiments on him. Did he still have powers? There was only one way to find out.

I'll focus my Earth powers on this wall, and I'll see if I can make a hole, he told himself flatly. He began by staring at the blank wall without blinking. His eyesight started blurring and losing focus due to the beam of reflecting walls. His eyes became the latest victims of snow-blindness, leaving him taken aback, and waiting for his sight to return. He thought of turning the walls to stone, so the light wouldn't be so blindingly intense.

Several minutes passed, and Ra'id's vision started coming up again. This time, he covered his eyes with his hand and placed the other on the wall. He wound back, then released with incredulous force. He then let energy flow from his body to his hand. A blunt crack was heard when Ra'id's palm connected with the wall. He lifted his hand to see the result. There stood a patch of earth cracked down the center, looking all rugged. It was about the size of a dinner plate, but remained to be attestation of his catalyzing abilities. He pulled back his arm to continue his work, but something queer stopped him from destroying the wall. The edges of the earth started to dissolve slowly, then headed inwards as if an acid had found corrosive material and started vaporizing the dirt.

Ra'id wouldn't give up. He glided his hand above the wall, letting water cascade from his palm. But, just like the earth, the water evaporated, until no evidence of existence remained. He slunk down against the cool surface of the wall, perplexed,

How is it that my powers aren't working here? Is it because I'm losing my strength, or something else is controlling it? He pondered his thoughts deeply for several hours. Something in his training brought a vague memory, poking him at the back of his mind.

All this thinking, however, was halted with an excruciating sting of hunger. His stomach started contracting over top of itself, and a strong burrowing feeling of a mole digging into his stomach started, until he squeezed upon it and waited. He looked around the bright room. Not one crumb of bread lay on the floor. Despite his hunger, Ra'id put his head on the cold floor and fell asleep.

*   *   *   *

"I know you know where we need to go, so why not tell me before I split your head like a MELON!!!" snarled Crenar, who arrogantly paced circles around Raghouik.

Crenar was clearly visible, for the sunlight had worked its way through the dust and webs of the dank room until it illuminated some of the wall. He wore a long starry robe, a ginger crown on his head lustrous with some of the rarest trinkets. In his right hand he had a glove of which he used to operate the Power Orb, and in the left hand he bore the Sklitificu Staff. The long rod was tarnished with some magical pigments, showing skeletons attacking enemies. The top was covered with three mystical objects, each with its own magical properties; the collar feather of the Gryphon, for fortification from unnatural Powers, the tail feather of the phoenix, giving the holder inexorable vigour, and finally the feather of a Hierocosphinx, which secured the holder's mentality from assaults. They lay attached by a string fixed into the staff.

King Crenar was growing very impatient that morning, as he was determined to find the whereabouts of the Blavarians, but Raghouik wouldn't give in,

"I will not tell you the whereabouts of my people, seeing you will be too greedy to kill them, but probably would leave them as slaves for eternity..." But as Raghouik saw the tip of the staff glow yellow, he added, "but if you kill me, you'll never know where it will be. And besides, why would my people want a master who compares his oppositions head with hard skinned fruit?" The glow died off and the staff returned to the ground, where Raghouik could see it. He was being held by his forearms by two heavy brutes, being forced into a kneel. Raghouik could've easily disposed of the guards, but one false move could end his life...

"I might want to kill you if you couldn't tell me... I have captured one of your apprentices just last night." Raghouik's expression suddenly turned from nonchalant to stunned. Crenar noticed this immediately, "So that does ring a bell, doesn't it? Well, we could have you destroyed, then get him to tell me..." Raghouik needed to find a way to fool him. Raghouik's expression remained unchanged.

"Well, if you think it's that easy, we'll just find someone to go and raid the fortress... I'm sure Sa'rin could tell me..." He rubbed his beard for a while, and then sent the guards off to take Raghouik back to his cell, stressing the 'Living' in 'Living room'. He sat back onto his untidy throne and relaxed himself.

*   *   *   *

"What was it that you wished to discuss~"

117

"Not so loud!" Said a hushed voice in the cluttered room. Though the closet was dimly lit, the people were easily distinguishable.

"Well, what is it?" Se'maj whispered.

"Ra'id can only cast the Dark spells even though I did not teach him because of the..." Se'maj held his breath, waiting under the suspense.

"The Gauntlet," Leinad said.

"The Gauntlet gives him power?"

"Yes. I couldn't tell him what happened to the Gauntlet; what made it Blavarix' enemy..." Leinad said guiltily.

"I don't know what happened! Spit it out!" Se'maj replied impatiently.

"When Blavarix himself created it, he used too much energy to make ~"

"Speak properly!" Leinad blurted out the secret:

"The Gauntlet is alive! It has a mind of its own! It has power beyond our vaguest dreams! And if it gets a strong hold on Ra'id, Xecwer itself would be mashed under its wrath!" Leinad said so melodramatically.

"Whoa, take it easy! Wouldn't it be more dangerous if Crenar got the Gauntlet?" Se'maj asked.

"Not at all. Crenar has a much stronger will than Ra'id. The Gauntlet will notice that and reject Crenar as a host. Even if it did accept Crenar as a proper host, Crenar's willpower will keep the Gauntlet's abilities useless," Se'maj was trying his hardest to keep up with Leinad's monologue,

"That's enough information for now, because anything could listening, for these days are different..."

Thud, thud, crunch...

It was deep in the night, and Ra'id slept uneasily. He lay curled up in a corner of the bright room. But instead of the blinding light, shadows flickered in the candle light. Ra'id suddenly woke up to a clanging of metal objects and the whirring of gears. He lifted his head slightly to get a glimpse of the source. His vision was blurred and couldn't see the thing, but its outline was clearly noticeable. Cerulean candlelight hit it from the right; its shape was roughly similar to one of a human. Once his vision came back did he notice his intruder. It was a Xecwerian with a navy visor wearing a jumpsuit shimmering with several symbols. Its figure hulked over Ra'id's intimidatingly. It had yet not noticed his victim was awake. Ra'id started plotting quickly,

3… 2… 1… Jump! Ra'id rose to his feet quickly. The creature shot several times with his machine. The ammunition collided with the wall and smashed into pieces. Ra'id scurried over to the other end, making sure he evaded each every bullet. He knew that the Xecwerian wasn't firing deadly bullets, but he would rather not find out the consequences of a clean hit in the arm. The fear in his stomach summoned his Gauntlet. In self defence, a clean mist shot from it, fogging the vision of the oncoming Xecwerian. If Ra'id was caught off his guard… let's just say we don't want him caught off guard. The being reached for his belt and retrieved a purple mass.

Plasma nets! Ra'id thought astonishingly. The fiend launched one at Ra'id, being careful not to lose balance. It whizzed past Ra'id and collided with the wall. A sickening splat was heard, and it echoed through the room.

He had to act fast. Ra'id ran up to the creature. He wasn't the most athletic person you could find, which gave his enemy plenty of time to sidestep from his line of fire.

If only I could get that gun… His gauntlet roused his powers alert. The monster launched his missile. This was not only accurate, but the torpedo seemed to slow as it approached him, yet he couldn't help but get hit.

Many thin needle-like arms hooked on to his skin, and began its duty. Ra'id didn't need to look at it; he could feel the mechanism doing its work. A sharp jab poked him on his arm, and he could feel his blood being sucked up slowly.

"Not on my watch!" He quickly sent a jolt of energy to his left shoulder. He quickly manipulated the jolt into stone. His arms grew rigid, and the machine simply limped off the rocky surface.

Ra'id was still running, gaining new momentum on his way with the earthy arm. The Xecwerian simply reloaded his gun, and fired. Ra'id embraced himself for the shot. One second... Two seconds... Nothing hit Ra'id. The intruder noticed that he was out of ammo. Ra'id made a burly fist of stone and whacked him. No. Whacked doesn't do justice to this hit. It was more like 'broke six or seven ribs with the mighty heave of fist of stone, weighing slightly less than a tonne'. But, no matter how you word it, the being laid crumpled in a heap of crushed bones and highly injured innards. For some reason, no one would've noticed that anything was broken from the outside.

Ra'id was exhausted due to the Gauntlet's extreme bloodlust, and had exaggerated the use of energy. He snatched the gun hastily, and his curiosity had awakened. The ammunition could have been valuable, but he tested its effect on the unconscious heap on the ground. He pocketed the man and found some more ammunition. He quickly loaded the gun and fired.

A round mechanism bolted out of the weapon, about the size of an apple and latched onto the fiend's clothes. Immediately, it started whirring, and began to spin around. A tiny blade dangled from the pod, grazing a cut against the garments. Then, the machine planted itself onto the bare skin. A siphon protruded into the hide, creating a thick hole. It then sucked up blood from it like a root of a plant. Ra'id glimpsed down disdainfully to the center of it. A clear piece of plastic kept the liquid inside, which showed a thick black fluid entering the chamber. The insides began spinning, removing the blood cells from the plasma. Suddenly, an amazing process began. The blood cells were being focused into a tube, which would be shaken, releasing all kinds of energy, and forcing the empty cells down. Pores opened through the side, letting the nutrients leak into a thin vial. The vial was then extracted from the pod and slid to Ra'id's feet.

He was stunned by the mechanism's actions. It repeated the process until it drained the creature of all its blood. The pod wilted; its mission completed. When Ra'id finally noticed it had stopped, he looked down at his feet. Thirteen vials lay there, looking untouched, and were filled with a scarlet liquid. It didn't appeal to Ra'id very much, but he knew that energy was stored there, ready for use. He turned over the immobile body of the foe and searched his equipment. There were several Plasma nets, a vest used to carry those tubes and several containers of ammunition.

Ra'id strapped the belt across his waist, but it was slightly larger. He picked up the vest and placed all of the tubes into the pockets, along with his firearm, and several Plasma nets.

Not bad. Even this slob was ready for anything.

As he grave-robbed the individual, he noticed a button. It was blue and had a case over top. Below, it read 'Dungeon Pass' in nicely stencilled letters. Ra'id pressed it in curiosity and hope of escaping this prison. Minutes passed in dead silence; nothing happened. All of a sudden, the walls all shook drunkenly, and cracks crawled across it. Then, a thin outline appeared, etching an entrance. Ra'id stepped towards it, and pushed the wall away with ease. A shimmering luminosity filled the room, and it beckoned Ra'id inwards.

Ra'id was drawn to the light, its contrast giving a warm and caring approach. It didn't burn his eyes like his cell had, but it regenerated him. Once Ra'id entered the room, the first thing he noticed was a man in tattered brown clothes lying limp on the cool floor. As Ra'id observed him, he noticed something very odd. He had five fingers, just like Ra'id, so he must've been human. He couldn't let the poor man suffer like that. As he drew nearer, Ra'id saw a thick blotch of blood running down his arm, indicating he was a victim of the leech-like mechanism he had found.

He reached into his vest and removed one of the vials. The liquid inside shimmered in the light. He removed the cork at the top and turned over the man. Ra'id let out a yelp. His face was scratched and torn, whip stains digging deep into his skin. It was covered in dirt and turmoil. His hair was wild and matted with blood. His eyelids showed many scars, and his mouth was thin. The nose was large and hooked over the mouth. Ra'id forced the man's mouth open and stuffed the vial in. Once the vial was drained, he waited for him to arouse himself. Soon, he started moaning and turning over. Ra'id forced another vial into his mouth. Immediately, his eyelids flew open. He got to his feet quickly and removed a dagger from his belt.

His teeth seem to be infected with some kind of a... yellowish puss! Not the greatest teeth,

"Tell me! Why are you here, young human? Tell me! I'll slice your neck if you don't!" He barked at Ra'id.

Neither is his breath... Thought Ra'id after getting a whiff. Now he knows how most dentists feel.

He backed away from the strange man,

"I'm from planet Earth, and I'm trying to escape this prison. I just wanted to know where I am ..." Ra'id threw nervous glances all over the room, trying to find some way to win the man over to his side. Then his eyes caught the empty vials scattered on the floor. He thought up something to say, "I'm the one who revived you! Look, those vials were the ones I gave you!" Ra'id grasped a vial, holding it high for the man to see.

"Oh, sorry then. It's just that these monsters come in every night to drain me," apologized the rugged man. His voice was nothing like his exterior. It was young and full of adventure. The man welcomed Ra'id to a corner of the room. He explained everything to Ra'id; the prison, and his identity.

"This prison is the Prison of Gillautinixe. This prison blinds the captives so they cannot escape. Most of the prisoners in here were capture by Signal Owls."

"Signal Owls?" Asked Ra'id, who couldn't grasp the thought.

"Yes. They befriend the enemies and send signals to Crenar with frequent hoots." Then Ra'id suddenly remembered his first day at the Blavarians,

"He was found talking to animals in the desert, and one was a Signal Owl."

"A Signal Owl?" Ra'id had asked.

"Yep. They work for Crenar, giving messages with their strange hooting. Don't be deceived by their cuteness,"

That owl that I welcomed into my friendship landed me here?! Ra'id couldn't believe how foolish he was, telling the owl everything, about the Blavarial Community and all. What was he to do? Crenar probably already knows the location by now. Ra'id slunk into the corner, a pang of guilt hitting hard in the stomach.

"I am Phelonius Cartatem, the trainer of heroes, the helper of the desperate, a wise hermit," Phelonius continued, "Here I'm known as…" He started mumbling before he could finish the sentence.

"What?" Ra'id didn't hear the last part quite properly. Phelonius realized what he said,

"Never mind…"

"Wait a minute! You trained heroes, as in, people in whom you saw great potential?" Demanded Ra'id.

"Well, my trainer told me so, and said he saw a great spark of life in me. He taught people how to smith weapons, and armour, and I was one of his early apprentices." He responded with much pride.

"Did you ever train Blavarix?" Questioned Ra'id, wondering if he was getting somewhere. Phelonius took a while to answer, thinking about what information to give.

"In a way I have, but my trainer trained him, mostly. He spoke most frequently about him…" he trailed off, then realised what information he was giving. He wouldn't continue, believing Ra'id might have been evil, but Ra'id thought hastily to give evidence.

"I know what he's done… I have his Gauntlet," He removed the glove from his left hand and showed the gauntlet. Its orange complexity shimmered in the warming light. The rings in the palm reflected against the wall. Phelonius gaped at the craft for several minutes, mesmerized by its swaying patterns.

"Look at the expert craftsmanship... the fine cutting... the rings... and the power..." Phelonius was holding the gauntlet by a finger. He could feel the ether radiating from it.

Ra'id finally withdrew the gauntlet; he had made his point. Phelonius snapped out of the hypnosis the minute it was moved,

"Well, I suppose you knew Blavarix,"

"Actually, and I'm sorry to say this, Blavarix was murdered by Crenar," Phelonius suddenly rose into rage,

"Murdered you say?" His voice became mystified, "Let me tell you this, boy," he crouched down to Ra'id's height and spoke in a more serious voice, "Things aren't always what they seem," he lowered his voice. He explained to Ra'id what had to be done, "I need to train you very well in blacksmithing, crafting and swordsman skills. You need to be the strongest ever before we can overthrow Crenar ~" He was cut of by Ra'id,

"Whoa! Wait a minute, old-timer! Aren't you jumping a bit far ahead? I haven't even seen Crenar and your planning our ploy now?"

"Why not?"

"Because I only have three or four days of training in – anything! And you fail to notice that were stuck in a prison cell, nowhere close to Crenar. When do you jolt our plan into action, might I ask?"

"Don't worry... The time will come..." Phelonius said most suspiciously. Ra'id rolled his eyes. I bet my sword he's bluffing. There's nothing much he can do in his state... There's nothing much I can do in this state – we're hopeless! Phelonius interrupted his truly negative thoughts,

"We must prepare now, for the time to attack approaches!" He said most theatrically.

"Must I put up with this? Read my lips: WE ARE HOPELESS!" He mouthed to Phelonius, but he seemed to have a flame that just wouldn't extinguish.

"Get off the floor!" Phelonius barked at Ra'id. He hastily got up from the ground. "I need you to focus. For the next several weeks, you will be training. No matter what it may be! From swords to craftsmanship, you'll know it inside out by the end of this month! Understood?" Ra'id whimpered before Phelonius,

"Yes, sir,"

"Do you have any special talents?" Phelonius spoke more quietly this time.

"I control the elements. Is that useful?"

"Of course it is!" He continued once more, "Well, with those powers, your will progress greatly indeed. Let's start with an anvil. I suppose you can make one with your abilities. Now, extend your arms towards the ground and awaken your earth powers," Ra'id felt the cold soil churn beneath him, and it sifted away until Ra'id had reached his goal; iron ore. He removed the iron from the ground as liquid, the shaped a small anvil.

"It's tiny, but it'll do." Ra'id reached into his vest and uncorked a vial. The liquid poured down his parched throat. A burning sensation seemed to fill him, and then he felt very energetic. He couldn't contain his energy, and he fought against the vitality from using his newly found energy. Phelonius continued, "We have no need for a furnace; you can use your energy to smelt the weapons. But for a hammer..." he reached into his rags, and pulled a large hammer from nowhere, big enough for crafting objects. He dug into his coat and pulled out a pair of pliers, then an old pair of gloves.

Does he have everything in that coat of his?

"I give these gloves to my apprentices, but I think you should use one, for the right hand," he tossed the brown glove which sagged over his hand. Ra'id removed his glove and replaced it with the old one. It seemed to fit perfectly.

"Now, for your first lesson. I will begin with metals and their properties," out of his clothes he pulled a small notepad. Another item from the coat. Ra'id noticed that the coat seemed smaller than before.

"Prepare to take rapid notes, and I'll explain the kinds of weapons made with specific metals," Ra'id opened the notepad in a rush, and found a pencil inside. He began with the title: 'Metal and their Properties'. He wrote so quickly, his words slurred off to the side. Without hesitation, Phelonius started gabbing quickly, on and on about corrosive metals, electrical metals, heavy metals, unstable metals, and various kinds of equipment,

"Electrical devices need the most active wiring, therefore I suggest gold, a very basic element and its conductivity is high. To create batteries for such devices, use many acidic compounds, and I suggest the metals einsteinium and fermium, they create a strong battery," he took a short pause, but Ra'id was trying to catch up. He didn't understand a single thing Phelonius had said, but he continued anyway, "Weapons can be made from metals such as Blavarite or Xecweranite, two very hard metals. But weapons you want to use to burn the opponent need to have a melted mixture of astatine to the Xecweranite. The weapons that have low air resistance need to be covered with a thin layer of liquid helium ~"

He was interrupted by a buzzing sound. Ra'id searched his vest and found the dungeon pass's button flashing blue. Dumbfounded, he pressed the button. A thin Xecwerian, his hair whitening with age, appeared instantly. Ra'id pushed the button again and an entry way opened. The man walked through silently, and the door closed.

The lesson droned on the same way for several hours. Ra'id had used several pages already, and was growing tired,

"Can we rest now?"

"Crenar isn't resting now," Phelonius shot back.

"Crenar isn't so bored that his eyeballs would pop out of their sockets…" Ra'id muttered under his breath. He had despised his first day of lessons.

Finally, night approached and the lights dimmed. Phelonius sent Ra'id off to sleep in that same compartment, making sure the equipment was well hidden. Ra'id fell to sleep once his head hit the hard floor. But Phelonius pondered his thoughts, trying to remember a very vague memory. Still not being able to get a hold of it, he returned to recollect the day's work. He planned for several weeks to teach Ra'id how to craft fine objects after being blacksmithed, and how to add special abilities to these seldom pieces of equipment. But for now, he slept uneasily, knowing the war would come.

*　　*　　*　　*

Chapter 12

The Blavarians hustled uneasily that day through the whole establishment. They knew that they had only several weeks before they would be forced into battle. It was simply logic to assume that Crenar had sent Sa'rin, and that she had already revealed the location of the Blavarians. Even though she had never reached Gillautinixe, evidence of Lay'tor's struggle clearly showed that an army had arrived. None had survived, but they had reached the location through Sa'rin's contacts.

Leinad was busy tearing his hair out of his head, trying to think of a way to hide the fact that the population would have to be sent to war. The remaining Chosen were out of the valley by then and were most likely in the Arid Waste along with Fisk and Na'yr. They were in search of the Power Orb, but, judging by the way the time that Ra'id was taking, he could only assume that he had been captured. Not only that, but he would be killed within a few weeks in the Prison. Leinad only had one choice to make: he clicked on his radio,

"Yes, sir?" Fisk's voice was discordantly heard through the speaker.

"Call off the mission. We need to ready the troops for the war of the century."

*   *   *   *

"Rise and shine, sleepy head! It's time to wake up! Breakfast is here," Ra'id rubbed his eyes and slowly rose from the ground. He was on the floor with an untidy notepad by his side, and a dulling pencil lying on the ground. He got up and walked to the wall where Phelonius was. His hair was as untidy as ever. He had left half of the crust of bread of the floor across from him.

A couple of weeks had passed. Seventeen days to be exact. Ra'id found it highly irregular to leave the prisoners sleeping on the floor. Most countries at least gave their prisoners a slightly elevated platform referred to as a 'bed'. Then again, they were prisoners of an egomaniacal tyrant king. They were lucky they had a toilet with some dividers for some privacy from the camera that was constantly poking its head out from the wall.

"I bet you that camera leads a way out…" Phelonius would always say whenever the mechanical whirring interrupted his lessons. Ra'id took the moments to rub his tired fingers with his Gauntlet. Blisters were already upon them due to writing with an infuriated temper.

"Today were actually going to do something practical, so you could leave your notepad in the corner over their," Phelonius pointed his crooked finger at the farthest corner away. He had done several lessons now, but each of them were studying metals. Today was something different, however. He was going to learn how to make a sword, starting from iron to steel.

Ra'id watched Phelonius nibble quietly on his small crust of bread. He had an aching pain in his stomach, so he wolfed down the minuscule piece of bread. Ra'id was getting used to eating a thin crust of bread twice a week in the morning, getting a short glass of murky water at noon, or so they thought. It was a small diet, but you could live with it for while.

He waited patiently for Phelionus to finish his bread, but hurried to the anvil to begin his work. "I'll ask you a question before we begin; do you know how a sword is smithed?" Asked Phelonius intently,

"It doesn't seem difficult. What you do is you heat up the bar of metal, and then pound it with your hammer until it's flattened. You then shape it into sword and wait for it to cool down." Ra'id waited for the verdict. Phelonius thought it over, and then noticed an obvious mistake,

"You got the first step right, and the second also, but the third was incorrect." He paused for a while, letting Ra'id correct his solution, "What has to be done is the sword needs to be folded in half by the pliers, then it's heated up again, nicked at the middle, then folded over. You repeat the same process, making sure the metal is folded the same way every time to layer it. Later, after about one thousand flips, the sword should be ready to be crafted." Ra'id couldn't believe his ears. One thousand folds!? That would take him over a day. Reading his mind, Phelonius answered him, "This assignment, if done well, should take you a bit over two weeks," he then added, "If you work all day."

Ra'id started right away. He retrieved his hammer, pliers and glove from the corner and brought it to his anvil to begin. But he forgot the most important part; iron. He knocked his earth powers awake when suddenly Phelonius handed his a heavy piece of iron, weighing roughly over thirty pounds. His arms were crushed under the weight. He lifted it to the anvil and started heating the bar lightly with his left hand. It suddenly turned bright orange, giving him a chance to pound it. His hammer left several uneven dents at first, but he got a good grip of it and started the right way. Once the bar grew thin, he pounded the middle by both its sides, allowing him to bend it over itself. The two metal pieces were red now, and they didn't seem to go in. He heated to a bright yellow, allowing the folded pieces to connect.

His shoulder ached for several hours, now being his tenth fold. The sword was becoming thinner now, and thin layers were seen from the side, allowing the sword to appear smaller, though it looked very similar to a tin foil sword. This toil continued until four o'clock in the afternoon, when Phelonius allowed Ra'id some rest. He took the crude blade and placed it under his cloak.

When Ra'id finally fell asleep, Phelonius conjured a medallion of Xecweranite, then produced some einsteinium and glazed the medallion. He then rested it on Ra'id, letting him sleep in peace.

*   *   *   *

The three children sat down in Leinad's office quietly, waiting for their dismissal. Yavin squirmed impatiently, however. He always had to be doing something. His thoughts let him meander all over the room. The shelves reached a high height of at least three meters. The bureau looked like a secretary's desk, but no computer of sticky notes lay stray on the counter. Instead, untidy sheets and loose papers were all scattered around the desk, leaving no open space. The window was yellowing with age; it appeared no one had cast any attention whatsoever towards cleaning it for several years.

Then Yavin saw it. Numerous crows pecked at the windowsill, staying put, as if they were observing the scene. It was awkward to see a murder of crows lay there, not cawing or fighting each other. Yavin examined them: head to toe. Then it struck him. A thin wire was attached to each foot. They were bugged!

Yavin sprung in action at once. He pounced at the window and fumbled with the lock on the window. Immediately, the birds flew off. This didn't stop Yavin. He summoned his electricity and sent several bolts of lightning down from the grey sky. Three birds were scorched, their bones fried into one unit. Two others escaped, flying off to the direction where Ra'id had chased Sa'rin.

"Yavin, what do you think you're doing? Those birds had ~" Leinad was stopped by Yavin,

"Everything to do with Crenar," before Leinad could counter him, he continued, "They were bugged." He picked one up with his magnetic powers and brought it to the window. On it was a crooked copper wire. Everyone was assembled by the window now. Leinad apologized to Yavin,

"I'm sorry to have accused you, but you did the best you could do. Those two escaped, and they're heading right to Crenar, where they'll tell him everything about the location. We need to assemble in the Dining Hall," a lady assistant walked in on queue and pulled a switch down from the wall. She then pressed a button and said,

"All Blavarians please assemble in the Dining Hall immediately," She walked away quickly to the hall. Everyone ran to the Dining Hall as fast as they could, before crowded groups flooded the hallway.

Once Leinad entered the room, everyone stopped whispering. They lay hushed, waiting for the news,

"I have more ill tidings. Maybe too much for some to bear. Just now a murder of King Crenar's crows was watching us, and they probably know our location," a sudden wave of murmuring filled the vast hall. Someone fainted and was held up by a neighbour from behind, "We must prepare for the war, for we do not know when they'll attack us. I'll ask all men over the age of fifteen to proceed to the arsenal arena." The silence ceased and everyone murmured, while some people rushed out towards the Training Grounds.

*   *   *   *

Living rooms are usually places where people gather together. Whether it's for a meeting of some sort, or there's a football game on TV, people of all ages interact in that room. That's how it's also adopted the name 'Family Room'. Whenever someone is asked to think of their living room or their family room, or even the 'Den', they'd think of a place where they usually spend time with their families. However not all 'Living' rooms were snug places where you can relax. Some times, the 'Living' room was where people hated going into. Most of the those people were rebels. Rebels of Crenar. So, when Raghouik was invited to the 'Living' room, this was not the warmest welcome. The 'Living' room was, of course, the living room. Literally.

Raghouik leaped over a cushion, evading large hands attempting to fling him into a gaping mouth at the end of the room. He was trying to escape the 'Living Room' for it was alive, and welcomed Raghouik into its presence. It had been several weeks for him in this room, ducking and dodging all over, making sure it couldn't catch him. He hadn't slept all month, making sure he wouldn't give in. The only source of food he had was the actual food for the living room, which was mainly scraps, but it kept him alive for a while.

When he had first entered, the room seemed quite peaceful. Two tiffany lamps on identical desks lit the room with a warm light. Leather sofas were symmetrically positioned in the room. Two, to be exact. Raghouik kept his guard up until he noticed a plump apple sitting on the desk, just waiting for someone to eat it. He walked past the sofas when he noticed something very peculiar. The rug before him was obviously Tuscan-made. Not that the expert rug had stopped him. It was just that the rug could only be from Earth, which was highly unlikely.

Something very strange also caught Raghouik's attention. He noticed that everything was, somehow, leaning towards him. It may have seemed insane to him if he were anywhere else, but Crenar was tricky and he knew that this was Crenar's scheme to get him killed.

One of the cushions suddenly twitched. Raghouik saw it was a trap. The creature, seeing that Raghouik was hesitant, lunged. The cushions uncurled themselves to make hands. The attempted to shovel Raghouik into the rug. The whole room jumped to life, each and every piece of furniture worked together as one unit. It was alive!

At the present time, Raghouik heard an abrupt rap on the door. Of course, it was useless because Raghouik was in no condition to answer a locked door. The guard, clearly noticing his errors, unlocked the door. The bolt slid back neatly. The furniture assumed its former position, for it did not want its secret to be unveiled. Raghouik, too, hid himself in the shadows in a corner away from the couch/hand. The steel door opened extremely noisily, for it hadn't been oiled in centuries,

"By King Crenar's order, you must see ~" a dark hand grabbed his throat and choked the words out of him in a high-pitched incomprehensible voice. There was no arm attached the hand. The guard tried to wrestle himself free, to no avail. After a quick minute, he passed out on the floor. Raghouik left the shadows and ran out of the room. The room would be alive in a few seconds, and he wanted to get as far away as possible. He bolted the door shut and ran free.

If a man were left in a room for a whole month, imagine how he'd feel running free in a fortress. He'd be pretty giddy. And, like a the giddy old man he was feeling like, Raghouik cried as he streak across the halls, in an extremely giddy tone,

"I'm free! I'm free! I'm ~" He tripped over his feet and face planted into the cobble stone floor. He scraped some sense into himself and noticed what he was doing. He got up immediately and stuck to the shadows. However, the shadow seemed a bit strange for a wall. But, Raghouik soon realized that this shadow was no corridor silhouette. He ran into something strong and solid that didn't feel like a cold wall.

A gigantic mountain of a Xecwerian grunted. The force itself left Raghouik squinting. The giant gave Raghouik a sharp tap to the head with his open palm. The hand could've curled around his skull. However, the hit knocked the absconder unconscious in a second, and the brute flipped his limp body over his shoulder to be bring him to his King.

Chapter 13

"I see, by the looks of it, you've survived the living room. Well, I have no need for you anymore, because I have the information I need," Crenar pointed towards the quiet owl, petting it with his hand, "Luckily this owl here told me everything." Raghouik wasn't listening at all; the thumping pain protruding his head kept him distracted and unaware of the environment around him.

Crenar left it that simple and with a snap of his fingers, he made Raghouik disappear. He felt as if he were being sucked through a thin rubber tube, the feeling not satisfying at all, considering the concussion he had received earlier, this wasn't his best day.

*   *   *   *

In Ra'id's quarters, he was busy finishing the last few folds on his sword, when his 'Dungeon Pass' started beeping. He easily pulled himself away from his tedious task and pressed the button. A blinding light flashed through the room. When the light dimmed, a dark shadow was hovering lightly above the ground. Its purple eyes seemed to sag a bit. Ra'id was about to press the button again when he noticed who it was. Raghouik stood, hovering weakly, waiting for his cell,

"Raghouik, is that you?" Asked Ra'id who approached him from the corner of the room.

"Ra'id? What're you doing here?" He asked in a weaker voice than Ra'id was used to. Nonetheless, he rasped just as much.

"Well, a signal owl tricked me and I ended up here. I was such a fool," he continued after bowing his head, "Now I know animals aren't to be trusted in this world." As the two friends greeted each other, Phelonius stood on the other side waiting. He suddenly remembered Raghouik and spoke up,

"Raghouik, is that really you? Remove your shadow." Raghouik's eyes turned towards Phelonius. His shadows slowly disappeared to reveal a middle age man with many scars crossing his face. His black hair was greying slowly, though his eyes seemed young. Ra'id didn't recognise him at all. His skin was dark, and suddenly Ra'id saw he was human; his hands had five thin fingers. He wore a dulling green tunic.

"Phelonius, I thought you were dead. Crenar killed you a while ago." Said Raghouik in a clearer voice.

"I vanished, but I didn't necessarily die," he held out his hand to Raghouik and gave him a pat on the back and said, "I'm back," Ra'id was completely confused. Who was this guy that Raghouik knew? He would have spoken about him at least. He simply resumed his sword, which was taking shape into a sharp blade. He heated and repeated the usual process, wondering why they didn't explain anything to him. He was lost and his mind was spinning.

Ra'id handed his finished blade to Phelonius, who was talking cheerily to Raghouik,

"Remember the Arachanecis, which turned out to be a warped illusion ~" they laughed, but when Ra'id tapped his shoulder, he stopped and said, "Well done. I'll finish the handle for you and add a little surprise... Anyway" and he continued with this ongoing jabbering.

Ra'id reached into his vest and pulled out his 'Dungeon Pass', and he pressed the button. His old cell opened, allowing him through. Many glasses of water and crusts of bread lay scattered on the floor. Retrieving them, he re-entered the usual cell and began the gorge. Raghouik and Phelonius joined the feast, knowing this would be a rare occasion. After they consumed the last crumb of bread, Ra'id asked a question,

"Raghouik, how do you know Phelonius?" Raghouik hesitated to answer. He walked quietly around the room, thinking it over. He gave a resentful look at Phelonius, who was busy with Ra'id's blade. Raghouik let out a long sigh, then whispered,

"I knew him as~" Phelonius cut him off and, under all the suspense, said,

"Ta-da! I finished your blade. The little thing that I added was a medallion of Moondust. If used carefully, your sword should swivel when danger is near. I also added silver studs to make it extra effective against dark beings," What used to be a bent-out-of-shape bar of iron was a darkened sword, with a gold handle and a golden-tinged circle rooted into the pommel.

Raghouik consulted Phelonius before telling Ra'id the truth. With a simple nod from Phelonius, he spoke up,

"As I was saying, I knew Phelonius as a blacksmith before we became friends. He was being trained by a wise man. Once his apprenticism was over, the trainer decided to retire and travel the world. Before he could do that, he vanished the night before. Then Crenar came into power and we started a small rebellion. We raided the fortress and retrieved the Power Orb. Shortly after that, we sent the Orb to Earth, knowing only humans could be bestowed with its power," The room grew silent after that, but Ra'id simply said,

"Crenar's human? How could he be? He…"

"Was the first human ever to set foot on this planet. When Xecwer was made, he descended from the heavens to keep the planet in order. The Orb followed and granted him powers."

"But who are you, Phelonius?" An awkward silence stilled the room. Knowing this was coming; he gave a long sigh and answered,

"Blavarix"

Chapter 14

At the Blavarial community, everyone was hustling faster than ever to get their equipment finished.

It's been a century or so since the last war, according to Se'maj. Some of the weaponry was in great condition. Most, however, was beyond repair. Therefore, the blacksmiths used the supply of Blavarite. Lemmor was silently sobbing in his office when he found out they used the entire supply.

Blacksmiths were all lined up at the storage room, waiting for their share of Blavarite. The line seemed never ending, but everyone got the metal. They began working immediately. Some groups would make swords, sizzling bright orange straight from the furnace.

The Xecwranite reserves were set aside for armour and shields. It seemed like the war was upon them in a week, because the need for metal rose by the minute. Leinad entered the fray to check their progress. A bright orange pile was gleaming to the left, awaiting crafters to add the finishing touch. A blue pile of blades without pommels were on the other side of the room.

Everything was in a blur; crafters were coming and going, taking many pieces of equipment, which they would piece together for a full suit of armour.

This stroll of Leinad's turned out to be a strenuous walk, as he waltzed into the training ground to assume the level of training, and to visit the battle animals frequently; it wouldn't hurt them to have a phoenix or a gryphon on their side. It all seemed so well until he saw Fisk running towards him,

"Lemmor's called an urgent meeting. Follow me." It didn't occur to Leinad that Lemmor calls these meetings when there's a difficulty up ahead. Their pace seemed rather slow, considering the fact the meeting was urgent, but Leinad didn't mind at all. Their destination was up ahead, now coming into view.

They opened the door of the bureau and entered without hesitation. Everyone in the room stopped talking to stare at them. The silence finally was subdued, and Leinad was given a summary of the plan,

"Okay, we'll have to start digging quickly through the underground; once we reach the battle field we can send our troops towards the grounds – oh Gir'heg, what's the status of the pods?" Lemmor asked Gir'heg as he walked in,

"All systems go! They're ready to launch at your command sir!" He saluted Lemmor and marched off. The children's heads were spinning, because they were confused by this whole meeting. Instead of intertwining themselves further, they simply kept their mouths shut and listened to the conversation,

"Leinad, we'll need you to lead the ground attack. Start the march today with the soldiers ready; we need to be there before Crenar." Leinad marched away in salute, hoping he had an easier task, "Tala and Yavin," they suddenly had awoken to their names, "You two will be joining Gir'heg on the aerial attack. He's the ranger, along with you two, so stay with him. He should be at the training grounds, readying the pods."

Following orders, the two of them rushed out of the room towards the Training grounds, making sure they picked up their weapons in their quarters. Yavin, however, dropped by Ra'id's room, just thinking that the predicament for the past several weeks was just a dream and Ra'id was really there. But as he opened the door, the silence remained as usual. He quickly grabbed Ra'id's Xecweranite scimitar, knowing he could use it during the war. After a long goodbye to his friend's dormitory, Yavin rushed out of the room.

"Sasha, you'll be lead by Fisk and Na'yr. Head towards the woman's dormitories to be escorted into your drill buggy." Totally confused, not knowing what a drill buggy was whatsoever, Sasha walked out of the room to her quarters, then to the woman's dormitories.

"Now that we've got everything settled," said Se'maj, "I would like Lemmor to go and wrap up the rest of the blacksmiths and crafters so they complete their work. Inform the trainers in the Training grounds to head towards the storage room for their armour." Lemmor was ushered out of the room to go complete his errands. Se'maj, as a veteran warrior many times, loaded his strap with tiny bullets full of molten lead. One shot could kill someone, and if not, then poison them. The strap contained at least one hundred of the bullets; his gun containing several more. He packed up a small cube, glowing from the top. It could minimize the size and mass of things put inside, allowing him to carry ammunition for everyone. It was a Mass Storage Device, and it would be useful in times like this.

He silently murmured to himself. He was long past his prime days. His bones creaked and moaned when he strung his gun across his chest. Luckily Lemmor would take over after this battle. Once it's all over, he could retire quietly and relax in the valley.

* * * *

"Okay, the coast is clear," beckoned Ra'id from the corner of the hall. He had his back glued against the wall, hidden by the shadows. Raghouik, Phelonius and Ra'id found that a crust of bread and a glass of infectious water wasn't enough food to support the three of them. They decided it was time to escape.

Phelonius had asked Ra'id to study the camera that probed inside the room every once and a while. Not the mechanism itself; he wanted him to study the angle of the camera.

It wasn't easy; Ra'id knew the camera, if it was similar to security cameras of Earth, emitted a faint laser. This laser was the where the camera focused. Of course, it's invisible to the human eye. However, Ra'id also knew that light could be slowed down. Though it travels at eighteen thousand miles per second in space. So, Ra'id, now knowing how to cleverly meld objects, created thin sheets of glass. It was crude at first, but Ra'id eventually developed a thin piece of glass, almost invisible.

After reproducing several copies, he stood the glass against the wall, with the help of some molten metal. Within the next hour, the camera popped out its head again to see the group. Phelonius noticed this and whispered,

"Remember what we rehearsed!" Raghouik nodded. He hid underneath the camera, away from its view. Ra'id had a stick and was drawing circles on the ground. Even though the camera could hear him he said,

"What'cha doin'?"

"Nuttin'," Phelonius said idiotically.

To the camera, it would've seemed like a child was drawing circles in the ground to avoid having his skull crack open from boredom. But, Ra'id was no normal child. He was simply acting like a child bored out of his mind. He was indeed, drawing circles in the ground. They marked the view of the laser, according to the glass panes that slowed it down significantly. They may have been slightly off (one could only eyeball a laser so well).

Phelonius walked out of the large circle that Ra'id was drawing and backed away against the wall. The next part was tricky, and the group only had a few minutes to perform the next operation. This needed to cause the camera to remain poking out from the wall while they operated on the base. Of course, Ra'id's brilliant plan and to locate the laser spot was baffled; the camera could be manually controlled from a central core, which is exactly what it did next.

The hydraulics of the camera whirred quietly. The lens retracted. The whole body rotated around the room. They started to panic silently. Phelonius hid his mouth from the camera, and mouthed,

"Plan B!" Raghouik wrapped his hand around the camera. Phelonius conjured a ring of titanium and placed it where the camera came out from the wall. Raghouik tore the machine from its wires. Sparks flew from the lacerated rod. The wall tried to close around the rod to seal up the room, but the titanium enforced ring get it open.

Ra'id reached inside the hole (while on Raghouik's shoulders, of course), and thrusted his fist around. He turned it to stone and punched a hole from inside the wall. Inside was the control room. A Xecwerian was shivering out of fright in the corner of the room, fumbling the controls. He called turned on his two-way radio and whispered,

"There's a breach in section E37. I repeat, a breech! Calling re-inforcement-" Static was on the other end. The Xecwerian looked up to see one shadowed figure who had ripped the wires right out of the sockets,

"Don't hurt me! Please! I have a family, you know!" Raghouik chuckled softly and hissed,

"Don't worry. I already paid for the funeral service." The next thing he remembered was a large shadow approaching his face a light speed.

Once they had exited, a pair of fit guards picked up a fight. However, they did not know their opponents were all Catalysts. Ra'id melted one to the wall, while Phelonius removed the other guard's armour, and Raghouik fuzzed his mind, making him think that the shadows were no longer still. Now, that guard was in the hallway, sucking his thumb and wishing the monsters would leave.

We come back to where our heroes were, as Ra'id beckoned his companions forward. The shadows kept them well hidden, considering the fact Raghouik could control them. Since they had to sidle often, their backs became very stiff and their necks started aching. It seemed like the maze would have never ended. As they round the corner stealthily, the hall opened into a vast room, where Ra'id had been in his dream several weeks ago. But instead of oddly shaped brutes, there was a winding line of people swerving across it. It took Ra'id several minutes to locate the beginning. Then he saw the Orb. Someone was holding for everyone else to touch in the line. The Orb seemed to be dead and didn't flash at all. Its blue aura fizzled and dimmed in the Xecwerians hands, and no one seemed to be having any affect on it,

"Raghouik, what're they doing?" Asked Ra'id, scared and curious at the same time,

"Well, Crenar wants to build an army, right? He thinks that his army should consist of Catalysts, but the only catalyst he has so far is himself, and he can't destroy everyone so easily, because we have quite a few Catalysts on our side," he leaned towards Blavarix, "so he's trying to see if anyone will be accepted by the Power Orb. Little does he know that only humans can be Catalysts." He showed his five-fingered hand compared to the other people's three-fingered hands.

So that's why the Power Orb looks unlively, thought Ra'id, and he waited for Blavarix's word,

"We'll have to pass through them to escape. Now, when I say go, you'll conceal the room with shadows-" he was cut off by a familiar rhythmic rumble, shaking the whole hall. He turned his head slightly to see a guard with his armour disfigured and eyes glowing red like hot coals of a fire. It stayed expressionless for a while. With unnatural agility, it swiped its clubbed hand across their heads, knocking them unconscious.

*   *   *   *

Chapter 15

Ra'id woke up, his head being thumped every so often by a fairly large bump protruding the back of it. He looked to his side when the pain subsided and saw the limp bodies of Blavarix and Raghouik. Trying to move towards them, he was cut short by a force pulling his neck against the ground. A slimy rasping voice echoed quietly throughout the room,

"Ahhh... have you come to see the show?" It said this so malevolently Ra'id couldn't bear it, "What's the matter? Is it because you can't move, being immobilized by my ultimate wrath? Well, you can't do anything about it now. My strength towers over your shrewd, insignificant power. I can stop anything you throw at me." Ra'id tried to open his mouth, but it was clamped shut by an invisible force. Crenar, however, knew he wanted to speak,

"My word, your vocabulary is bordering beyond horrific. I daresay, you don't seem like much of a threat to me." Rage had built inside of him. Without hesitation he released it, its target; Crenar's heart. Not a single cry of pain was released,

"Ah, very good... I see you understand your limits," His slippery voice still didn't disappear for he was still alive. Ra'id tried to throw more fire, and let the rage build up. But he suddenly realised what Crenar wanted. He wanted Ra'id to use his energy, making him useless for a battle.

A wave of energy flew over Ra'id. His limbs were no longer numb. Leaping to his feet, he tried to rouse Blavarix. Suddenly, a strange barrier forced him back into a rocky chair,

"No, no, no. you, mustn't go and wake them up. Let them enjoy the last rest they'll ever have," hissed Crenar. Ra'id couldn't even throw a quick glance at him; the force was overwhelming. In attempt to stop the force, he took all the oxygen around Crenar to suffocate him. But a might kept the air held back, leaving Ra'id's powers useless,

"What are you trying to do? Your powers are no match compared to the feather of the Gryphon, which shields me from unnatural Powers. The best you could do now is sword-fight me to the death, but you couldn't stand a chance against me; this phoenix feather gives me strength beyond compare. There's nothing left for you to do,"

"How long did it take you to remember all of that?" Ra'id said, stalling for as much time as possible. Crenar scoffed,

"Words are all you have now." The tip of his staff suddenly glowed white, blinding Ra'id. As he released the energy from the staff, Blavarix suddenly had awoken. He shot himself straight upright, and stopped the force. Ra'id was freed from his bind and the beam of light struck the chair he was sitting on, leaving a dusty crust behind, "I was surprised to have seen you again; I thought the prison would have killed you," said Crenar as casual as ever,

"You underestimate me, and don't understand my power. I challenge you to a Catalyst's duel," Crenar flinched at the word 'catalyst'.

"It'll be my pleasure, Blavarix, to beat you in this duel," They backed away several paces from each other. Crenar suddenly enlarge the room, enhancing the battle field. Blavarix made some rules,

"That staff can't be used; I know it blocks any unnatural Powers," Crenar cast aside his Sklitificu Staff without care. Ra'id winced as the priceless artefact clacked along the ground.

"But I have some rules too," claimed Crenar, "You can't kill the opponent immediately; only if they've been knocked to the ground, and you can't use your glove thingamajig," He finished, but as he glanced to the side he said, "Ah, yes. I almost forgot," he moved aside the wall to leave a large spacious area, allowing them to see the outside of the building.

There were millions of Xecwerians wearing orange armour. Two groups were divided; one lay to the right, another to the left. The group to the left carried a large banner with a glowing glove etched on to it. Everyone could tell that side was of the Blavarians; the glove was the Gauntlet of Blavarix. To the right was a group of hulking figures, some of them concealed by shadows and others to large to be wearing armour. Crenar's army outnumbered Blavarix's two to one. It seemed most unlikely the Blavarians were to succeed at all, "I just wanted everyone to see their ruler die before them," continued Crenar, and Ra'id's attention fell back to them. They stood there, at the ready, facing each other sternly like statues. But Crenar removed an obstacle from his path to victory; Ra'id was teleported into the battlefield, with only a studded blade. Crenar murmured the solitary word that would begin both the war and their duel, "Begin".

Everyone in the field let out harsh war cries. The left side had blue weapons, while some had large, metallic guns that pulsed lively. It took a minute or two before the two groups collided. But once they did, the assembly to the left flickered, and then vanished. Ra'id, however, stood at the back of the group, holding his iron scimitar studded with silver. The other side stood there, dumbfounded, not knowing where the opponents had disappeared. Suddenly, the ground before them broke away, and a large twelve wheeler truck rose from it, with a drill at the front, whirring at top speed. Several more of these buggies appeared. Out of them jumped several groups of people, all armoured and ready for battle. They sliced past the first wave of Crenar easily. The second one came forth, a clad of men with several neutrino powered catapults. Another sneak attack came forth, as arrows rained from the sky. Not only that, but a phoenix flew by the falling arrows, throwing blue flames at them. Ra'id recognized the grey tuft of hair behind the neck of the phoenix; Tala. Dozens of oval shaped helicopters descended from the sky, containing hundreds of men each. The torrent of arrows continued, and several plasma nets had been thrown. The battle had truly commenced, and Crenar's army had already lost its first three waves.

"I see Ra'id!", yelled Yavin from one of the pods. The whirling helicopter blades beat on Yavin's ear drums. The helicopter slowly descended, and Yavin jumped from it as it approached the earth. Ra'id jumped when he heard a thud land beside him. He shot a glance to his right and saw Yavin,

"Ah, you've come to join the battle?" He said calmly as he parried a hobgoblin's club. He quickly swivelled his sword through the armour, reaching the flesh. The studs pierced it, and the fiend fell back, rolling in agony. Seconds later its flesh became rocky. It attempted to get up, but crumbled into small particles of dust, "Now I know the power of silver!" Ra'id and Yavin fought back to back, the groups surrounding them quickly. Though Yavin was a ranger, he fought pretty well with his katana. He had drawn the thin blade of steel and was parrying carefully. When he connected with armour, electricity from within would reduce his adversaries into measly piles of dust. A whirlwind picked up, blinding the two companions as they swung their swords randomly into space. It subsided most suddenly, and the Ra'id could open his eyes. One of the pods had landed beside them and Gir'heg was at the wheel,

"Hurry up or you'll be werewolf food!" Yavin and Ra'id ushered themselves into the pod hastily, dodging low arrows whizzing through the air.

Inside, the two of them took a few gulps of air sitting back in the relaxing pod.

"Ra'id, I have your armour, and Yavin took the trouble into bringing your blade," Gir'heg pointed to a bundle of armour placed behind his seat. It took a while for Ra'id to piece it together, but once it was made, he felt protected inside,

"I need to add these silver studs to my sword," he let out his rage. That was enough to blow Ra'id into flames. But he calmed himself and controlled his anger. By doing so he was able to remove the studs with minimal heat, and then replace them onto his blade. They looked oddly smeared, but it was enough to kill the ghouls. He quickly removed the medallion from the pommel and fused it into the middle of his scimitar. It glowed with life when it was replaced. His gauntlet jived in his hand, and it was glad to be back with the scimitar. He didn't grab for a shield. But before Ra'id exited, he noticed a pulsing neon blue column of energy.

"What's that?" He asked, pointing to it.

"Neutrino energy," Gir'heg replied.

Heat flew into the pod and he walked out, armoured and all. It made his movements sluggish, but the protection was worth it. He ran out to join the battle. Yavin was still in the pod trying to shoot at the enemies below. Tala was severing several guards with his large scythe-like claws. Ra'id hurried into the crowd, and saw a large Minotaur wielding a heavy axe of iron. Though the blade was soft compared to the Blavarian's armour, the actual thrust left some heavy damage. The poor victim shielding himself from the blows was none other than Leinad. Ra'id charged into the fight, sheathing his blade. The Minotaur could bend Ra'id's sword like a toothpick, so the elements were his only chance. He grew a rage inside him, but the Minotaur obviously sensed him. It turned towards Ra'id. Immediately, his ambush was ceased. He felt a cold fear crawling up his spine. His gauntlet acted most bizarrely and shot a thick stream of cold water towards the beast. The Minotaur's bull head was engulfed, and coated with a thick Ra'id had quickly thrust his silver dagger into the belly of the Minotaur. This didn't have the same effect as it had on the Hobgoblin, but the Minotaur still fell over, holding its bleeding stomach. Leinad finally got up from the ground, one of his blades mangled by the Minotaur's axe. Without thanking him, Leinad rushed off to fight another opponent.

In the building, a silent battle was taking place. Crenar waited patiently for Blavarix to attack. Blavarix kept on sending a wide diversity of metals, each being deflected off an invisible force field,

"Don't meddle with the forces of space..." whispered Crenar. He didn't seem nervous one bit. Blavarix could see his technique wasn't working.

Arsenic is a powerful poison against enemies, and I should caution you to use it only on enemies; not on rivals, but strictly enemies... Blavarix recalled a lesson where he taught Ra'id about poisonous metals. He swiftly shot powdered arsenic from his hands. It seemed to fall like black soot from above Crenar. He didn't seem to notice the soot, but the effects were immediate. All of a sudden, his arms fell down to his side; his energy wasn't being made, because arsenic contaminated his body. It would be several minutes before he died. Crenar didn't give in, however, and fed himself energy through space itself. He had shrunk the universe from its enormous size, took a fraction of it away and allowed the energy to flow in. Then, he removed the soot from his lungs, making his spatial powers act benignly for once. Crenar was back at full force now, and he continued the battle. This time he attacked aggressively, shooting waves of seismic shock waves to tear Blavarix apart. Agile and swift, Blavarix jumped out of the way of them, paying his utmost attention towards them. Wasting no time, Crenar seized his chance.

The battle below them seemed to rage on. A number of blue blades were scattered on the ground. Bodies covered even more of it, however. Crenar's strength was quantity; Blavarix's was quality. Quite a few gryphons had joined the fight for freedom, and they picked up many Xecwerians and tossed them aside. The rangers from the cliffs were dominating the field; most of the deaths had been their cause. Sword met shield, and the battle raged on. Sasha used her sari'kun to splice enemies in two, which worked quite effectively. Yavin was busy ranging from above the cliffs, shooting electric arrows. They glided further than most of the usual arrows, not to mention faster. Tala was busy commandeering the gryphons to attack the opposition. She would transform often into a phoenix, harpy or gryphon, and would gleefully fly opponents away to a cliff far away from there, and drop them to their death. Ra'id, however, had encountered a giant clad of warriors of Crenar's, and they all had protection from his elements. Crenar had taught them how to reduce the powers of the Catalysts, no doubt. Ra'id no longer let his weakened powers take advantage of him. He drew his blade quickly, when suddenly the air grew chilly. The soldiers looked about, unable to find the source, but Ra'id's blade writhed wildly in his hand. It slipped from his palm and landed a few feet from him. Right in front of it stood a scrawny looking sleepless werewolf. It wasn't night, so this wasn't an ordinary wolf. It was a Lupo Manare, which was a wolf at first, then became part human later on. They were very vicious, according to one of the lessons Ra'id was taught by Leinad,

"Whenever you come across a Lupo Manare, don't run, but walk away slowly,"

"But what's the difference between it and a werewolf?" Asked Ra'id, confused.

"Lupo Manare transforms from wolves, and only during the day, everyday, and has a vicious appetite. The only way a wolf is to become one is by making a blood sacrifice to a witch…"

"Huh? They exist?" Leinad paused, and didn't quite answer,

"Never mind. As I was saying…"

Ra'id finally came back to Xecwer, and he was still face to face with the vicious wolf. It looked like a man with an arched back. The spine was easily seen through the thin layers of skin. The hair was short and thin, mostly grey, and parts here and there matted with blood. The jowls of the beast were pointed and fitted neatly into one another. Scarlet saliva oozed from the bottom lip, and the snout was short and rectangular. The nose remained black, but the arms hung lazily at its side. Its legs were in a half kneel, and the ankles were quite long. A short stub of a tail remained on its back. The ears were beside the eyes, and looked floppy. The left eye was green, while the other was yellow. Ra'id lifted his head slightly from the ground to see the snarling face of the beast, looking down at him. It shot fear into Ra'id, but even his gauntlet wouldn't release a freezing blast this time. The gauntlet decided to let Ra'id do the fighting. The Lupo pulled back one arm and swung it back. The strength of it sent Ra'id several meters back, and he face planted into the ground. Some of the guards chuckled, but that was silenced by a snarl from the wolf. It walked up to Ra'id, who attempted to retrieve his sword from his sheath, but it wasn't there. Not wasting anymore time, the half wolf snarled and its steps became louder. Ra'id could here it coming and his could sense the air growing colder. As he awaited his fate, a cold blade pressed against his stomach. His dagger! He reached for it, turned from the ground, and he jumped off. He let the blade lead the way through the air, and it reached its target; Lupo's heart. Before the wolf could fall back, its body crumbled to dust, just like the Hobgoblin's had.

He retrieved his sword with his air abilities and diced several unwary guards in two. The smirks vanished from their faces, and they retreated. A clear path laid for him to enter the castle, and he charged for it. Warriors didn't seem to notice him charging in a full clad of armour, but it did drag him back. His anger against Crenar slowly reflected himself outside, and his armour melted away. The metal was valuable, but it wasn't worth Blavarix' life. He gained a new speed, and sprinted up the musty staircases.

Guards didn't patrol the halls due to the commotion unravelling from outside. Ra'id found it difficult to navigate through the winding paths. It was a maze. He finally reached a fork and took a moment to catch his breath. He couldn't decide which one to take, but thought it out in his mind,

Right or left? Right or left…his thoughts were broken when his sword sheath started pulling him forward. He unsheathed the blade, letting it lead the way. It stopped at the fork and seemed to decide the direction to take. It swivelled right, and then left. It suddenly started whirling uncontrollably, forcing Ra'id into a spin. It stopped quickly at the right, attempting to stand still, but it remained fidgety. Wasting no more time, he ran in that direction, holding his dagger in his hand and the sword pulling him along.

Crenar had finally bound Blavarix to the ground with an extreme pulse of gravity and was about to kill him that instant. He drew his blade happily from its sheath. Cherishing this moment, he waited a few seconds. As he prepared to drop the blade, Ra'id ran into the room. He knocked the blade aside with a compressed vortex. Ra'id stared at the predicament, knowing he had little chance to save Blavarix. Crenar smiled maliciously at Ra'id's entrance and simply said,

"About time you dropped by, Ra'id..." Ra'id was stunned. He didn't remember telling anything to Crenar about his name. The gauntlet again shot mud at Crenar, who blocked the splatter and cast it aside, "Don't you dare throw mud at me!"

Crenar stood up from Blavarix, and rage seemed to build into, as his nonchalant tone faded away like a long lost dream. Crenar didn't reach for his staff to kill Ra'id; his blade would've done just as well. He raised his hand to give Ra'id his eternal destiny, but Ra'id simply stood there, courage filling his inner self. He got up from the ground, and looked Crenar straight in the eye. Crenar tried to look away from the deep stare. His courage heated up the air, causing Crenar to sweat, but the earth suddenly stirred too,

"The only reason why you have so much power is because no one was strong enough to stand up against you. Not one. Except for Blavarix. He's the only one with enough courage to keep his rights, enough courage to fight for freedom,"

"I've let my people have freedom, you fool! They can have all the freedom they want! Don't you dare question my authority!" Ra'id, however, didn't care about Crenar's babbling,

"You call that freedom?!" He cried angrily at the large force field separating them from the war taking place outside. The ground was muddy now, but it hadn't rained. There was a scarlet mixture oozing out of everybody that had paid the price of a search for 'freedom'. Ra'id now stood face to face, his shoulders raised, his temper rising quickly. As he breathed, the temperature in the room followed. He inhaled and it went up; he exhaled and it went down. Crenar stood in front of his throne, frozen with fear.

As the elements grew wild in the chamber, Raghouik was waking up slowly. He stirred from the ground, and saw Ra'id walking up to Crenar. He thought he was dreaming, and simply let the matter fall away. But to Ra'id, it wasn't a dream. He could feel his emotions switching beyond control. Vengeance seemed to have taken over, and already lava was seeping from his hands, heading towards Crenar. The air grew humid, and thick droplets started forming. First on Ra'id's forehead, then in the air. A dark cloud lingered above the two of them, and a small crackle was heard. The humidity and the heat clashed, and a large funnel spiralled down from the cloud. A cyclone billowed vigorously. Ra'id tried to hold back his energy, but couldn't.

Raghouik regained his senses and yelled out,

"Ra'id, don't!" Ra'id stopped and turned with a shrug. Immediately, Crenar plunged his sword in Ra'id's stomach.

"No!" Blavarix called out. Ra'id fell to the ground, the sword in his stomach. He was brutally wounded, his eyesight spinning. The pain didn't last, but his senses started fading.

He looked at his hand. A crimson stain was on the gauntlet. Suddenly, Ra'id felt that feeling of the gauntlet taking over. His hand started moving, writhing all of a sudden. Then, the glove popped off and started crawling away from Ra'id. The parasite saw that it's host was dying.

"Get that bug!" Raghouik called at the gauntlet slowly creeping towards the stairs. Blavarix was too busy fighting. He'd gotten up and attacked Crenar. Immediately, he disappeared. Ra'id suddenly understood why the gauntlet couldn't come off. He was hostage to a parasite, and it didn't want the host to die, therefore taking control and protecting him. It was out of sight now, probably seeking another inattentive host.

Ra'id's vision slowly faded away. He could only hear; his other senses had vanished too. He could only hear several words. Inaudible at first, they made no sense,

"Wake up…"

Wake up? Ra'id thought lazily, what do they mean?

"Wake up! You'll be late for school!" Reminded Ra'id's mother from downstairs. Ra'id got up from the sleeping bag.

Only a dream? What?! I could've… I could've… He started pulling his hair off of his head.

"Ra'id, are you feeling all right?" Yavin asked suspiciously. Realizing what he was doing, Ra'id said,

"Uh, I'm fine," Sasha had this are-you-sure sort of face glaring at Ra'id.

"Honestly, I'm fine!"

They got dressed, brushed their teeth and packed their bags. They hurried down stairs and wolfed down their breakfasts of pancakes and sausages smothered in creamy maple syrup, and headed out the door with Ra'id's mother. They jammed themselves into the minivan, and got out of the driveway. Ra'id felt like something was missing. He checked his bag for everything.

Pencils… Notebook… Binder… Textbook… Homework… He wasn't missing his homework this time. He sighed heavily. Only another dream that lead up to another boring day at school. He laid his hand on his stomach and gazed out the window.

Boring… he thought. Suddenly, he stomach felt a stinging pain, like hot needles on it. He rolled up his shirt, wondering what the source of the pain was. And there it was. A red cut scourged across his belly, stitched together, where a sword had struck.